I0599473

Ruth McEnery Stuart

In Simpkinsville

Character Tales

Ruth McEnery Stuart

In Simpkinsville
Character Tales

ISBN/EAN: 9783743348820

Manufactured in Europe, USA, Canada, Australia, Japa

Cover: Foto ©Andreas Hilbeck / pixelio.de

Manufactured and distributed by brebook publishing software (www.brebook.com)

Ruth McEnery Stuart

In Simpkinsville

[P. 68

"'I'M MIGHTY GLAD YOU'VE SPOKE'"

IN SIMPKINSVILLE

Character Tales

BY

RUTH McENERY STUART

ILLUSTRATIONS BY

SMEDLEY, CARLETON, AND McNAIR

NEW YORK
HARPER & BROTHERS PUBLISHERS
1897

CONTENTS

ILLUSTRATIONS

AN ARKANSAS PROPHET

A NEW-YEAR'S STORY

AN ARKANSAS PROPHET

IF you would find the warmest spot in a little village on a cold day, watch the old codgers and see where they congregate. That's what the stray cats do, or perhaps the codgers follow the cats. However that may be, both can be depended upon to find the open door where comfort is. They will probably lead you to the rear end of the village store, the tobacco-stained drawing-room, where an old stove dispenses hospitality in an atmosphere like unto which, for genial disposition, there is none so unfailing.

From November to May the old stove in the back of Chris Rowton's store was, to its devotees at least, the most popular hostess in Simpkinsville. And, be it understood, her circle was composed of people of good repute. Even the cats sleeping at her feet, if personally tramps, were well connected, being lineal descendants of known cats belonging to families in regular standing.

Many, indeed, were natives of the shop, and had come into this kingdom of comfort in a certain feline lying-in hospital behind the rows of barrels that flanked the stove on either side.

It was the last day of December. The wind was raw and cold, and of a fitful mind, blowing in contrary gusts, and throwing into the faces of people going in all directions various samples from the winter storehouse of the sky, now a threat, a promise, or a dare as to how the new year should come in.

"Blest if Doc' ain't got snow on his coat! Rainin' when I come in," said one of two old men who drew their seats back a little while the speaker pushed a chair forward with his boot.

"Reckon I got both froze and wet drops on me twix' this an' Meredith's," drawled the newcomer, depositing his saddle-bags beside his chair, wiping the drops from his sleeves over the stove, and spreading his thin palms for its grateful return of warm steam.

"Sleetin' out our way," remarked his neighbor, between pipe puffs. And then he added:

"How's Meredith's wife coming on, doctor? Reckon she's purty bad off, ain't she?"

The doctor was filling his pipe now and he did not answer immediately; but presently he said, as he deliberately reached forward and, seizing the tongs, lifted a live coal to his pipe:

"Meredith's wife don't rightfully belong in a doctor's care. She ain't to say sick; she's heart-broke, that's what she is; but of co'se that ain't a thing I can tell her—or him, either."

"This has been a mighty slow and tiresome year in Simpkinsville," he added in a moment, "an' I'm glad to see it drawin' to a close. It come in with snow an' sleet an' troubles, an' seems like it's goin' out the same way—jest like the years have done three year past."

"Jest look at that cat—what a dusty color she's got between spots! Th' ain't a cat in Simpkinsville, hardly, thet don't show a trace o' Jim Meredith's Maltee—an' I jest nachelly despise it, 'cause that's one of the presents *he* brought out there—that Maltee is."

"Maltee is a good enough color for a cat ef it's kep' true," remarked old Pete Taylor—"plenty good enough ef it's kep' true; but it's like gray paint—it'll mark up most anything it's mixed with, and cloud it."

"I reckon Jim Meredith's Maltee ain't the only thing thet's cast a shade over Simpkinsville," said old Mr. McMonigle, who sat opposite.

"That's so," grunted the circle.

"That's so, shore ez you're born," echoed

Pete. "Simpkinsville has turned out some toler'ble fair days since little May Meredith dropped out of it, but the sun ain't never shone on it quite the same—to my notion."

"Wonder where she is?" said McMonigle. "My opinion is she's dead, an' thet her mother knows it. I wouldn't be surprised ef the devil that enticed her away has killed her. Once-t a feller like that gits a girl into a crowded city and gits tired of her, there's a dozen ways of gittin' shet of her."

"Yas, a hundred of 'em. It's done every day, I don't doubt."

"See that stove how she spits smoke. East wind 'll make her spit any day—seems to gag her."

"Yas," McMonigle chuckled softly, as he leaned forward and began poking the fire, "she hates a east wind, but she likes me—don't you, old girl? See her grow red in the face while I chuck her under the chin."

"Look out you don't chuck out a coal of fire on kitty with your foolin'," said old man Taylor. "She does blush in the face, don't she? An' see her wink under her isinglass spectacles when she's flirted with."

"That stove is a well-behaved old lady," interrupted the doctor; "reg'larly gits religion, an' shouts whenever the wind's from the right quarter—an' I won't have her spoke of with disrespect.

"If she could tell all she's heard, settin' there summer and winter, I reckon it 'd make a book—an' a interestin' one, too. There's been cats and mice born in her all summer, an' birds hatched; an' Rowton tells me he's got a dominicker hen thet's reg'larly watched for her fires to go out last two seasons, so she can lay in her. An' didn't you never hear about Phil Toland hidin' a whiskey bottle in her one day last summer and smashin' a whole settin' o' eggs? The hen, she squawked out at him, an' all but skeered him to death. He thought he had a 'tackt o' the tremens, shore—an' of a adult variety."

"Pity it hadn't a-skeert him into temperance," remarked the man opposite.

"Did sober him up for purty nigh two weeks. Rowton he saw it all, an' he give the fellers the wink, an' when Pete hollered, he ast him what was the matter, an' of co'se Pete he pointed to the hen that was kitin' through the sto'e that minute, squawkin' for dear life, an' all bedaubled over with egg, an' sez he: 'What sort o' dash blanketed hens hev you got round here, settin' in stoves?' And Rowton he looks round and winks at the boys. 'Hen,' says he—'what hen?

Any o' you fellers saw a hen anywhere round here?'

"Of co'se every feller swo'e he hadn't saw no hen, an' Rowton he went up to Pete and he says, says he: 'Pete,' says he, 'you better go home an' lay down. You ain't well.'

"Well, sir, Pete wasn't seen on the streets for up'ards o' three weeks after that.

"Yas, that stove has seen sights and heard secrets, too, I don't doubt.

"They say old nigger Prophet used to set down an' talk to her same ez ef she was a person, some nights, when he'd have her all to hisself. Rowton ast him one day what made him do it, and he 'lowed thet he could converse with anything that had the breath o' life in it. There is no accountin' for what notions a nigger 'll take.

"No, an' there's no tellin' how much or how little they know, neither. Old Proph', half blind and foolish, limpin' round in the woods, getherin' queer roots, and talkin' to hisself, didn't seem to have no intelligence, rightly speakin', an' yet he has called out prophecies that have come true —even befo' he prophesied about May Meredith goin' wrong.

"Here comes Brother Squires, chawin' tobacco like a sinner. I do love a preacher that 'll chaw tobacco.

"Hello, Brother Squires!" he called out now to a tall, clerical old man who approached the group. "Hello! what you doin' in a sto'e like this, I like to know? Th' ain't no Bibles, nor trac's for sale here, an' your folks don't eat molasses and bacon, same ez us sinners, do you?"

"Well, my friends," the parson smiled broadly as he advanced, "since you good people don't supply us with locusts and wild honey, we are reduced to the necessity of eatin' plain bread an' meat—but you see I live up to the Baptist standard as far as I can. I wear the leathern girdle about my loins."

He laid his hand upon the long leather whip which, for safe-keeping, he had tied loosely around his waist.

"Room for one more?" he added, as, declining the only vacant chair, he seated himself upon a soap-box, extended his long legs, and raised his boots upon the ledge of the stove.

"I declare, Brother Squires, the patches on them boots are better'n a contribution-box," said McMonigle, laughing, as he thrust his hand down into his pocket. "Reckon it'll take a half-dollar to cover this one." He playfully balanced a bright coin over the topmost patch on the pastor's toe.

"Stop your laughin', now, parson. Don't shake

it off! Come up, boys! Who'll cover the next patch? Ef my 'rithmetic is right, there's jest about a patch apiece for us to cover—not includin' the half-soles. I know parson wouldn't have money set above his soul."

"No, certainly not, an' if anybody 'd place it there, of co'se I'd remove it immediately," the parson answered, with ready wit. And then he added, more seriously:

"I have passed my hat around to collect my salary once in a while, but I never expected to hand around my old shoes—and really, my friends, I don't know as I can allow it."

Still he did not draw them in, and the three old men grew so hilarious over the fun of covering the patches with the ever-slipping coins that a crowd was soon collected, the result being the pocketing of the entire handful of money by Rowton, with the generous assurance that it should be good for the best pair of boots in his store, to be fitted at the pastor's convenience.

It was after this mirth had all subsided and the codgers had settled down into their accustomed quiet that the parson remarked, with some show of hesitation:

"My brothers, when I was coming towards you a while ago I heard two names. They are names that I hear now and then among my people—names of two persons whom I have never met—persons who passed out of your community some time before I was stationed among you. One of them, I know, has a sad history. The details of the story I have never heard, but it is in the air. Scarcely a village in all our dear world but has, no matter how blue its skies, a little cloud above its horizon—a cloud which to its people seems always to reflect the pitiful face of one of its fair daughters. I don't know the story of May Meredith—or is it May Day Meredith?"

"She was born May Day, and christened that-a-way," answered McMonigle. "But she was jest ez often called Daisy or May—any name thet 'd fit a spring day or a flower would fit her."

"Well, I don't know her story," the parson resumed, "but I do know her fate. And perhaps that is enough to know. The other name you called was 'Old Proph',' or 'Prophet.' Tell me about him. Who was he? How was he connected with May Day Meredith?"

He paused and looked from one face to another for the answer, which was slow in coming.

"Go on an' tell it, Dan'l," said the doctor, finally, with an inclination of the head towards McMonigle.

Old man McMonigle shook the tobacco from his pipe, and refilled it slowly, without a word.

Then he as deliberately lit it, puffed its fires to the glowing point, and took it from his lips as he began:

"Well, parson, ef I hadn't o' seen you standin' in the front o' the sto'e clean to the minute you come back here, I'd think you'd heerd more than names.

"Of co'se we couldn't put it quite ez eloquent ez you did, but we had jest every one of us 'lowed that sence the day May Meredith dropped out o' Simpkinsville the sky ain't never shone the same.

"But for a story? Well, I don't see thet there's much story to it, and to them thet didn't know *her* I reckon it's common enough.

"But ez to the old nigger, Proph', being mixed up in it, I can't eggsac'ly say that's so, though I don't never think about the old nigger without seemin' to see little May Day's long yaller curls, an' ef I think about her, I seem to see the old man, somehow. Don't they come to you all that-a-way?"

He paused, took a few puffs from his pipe, and looked from one face to another.

"Yas," said the doctor, "jest exactly that-a-way, Dan'l. Go on, ol' man. You're a-tellin' it straight."

"Well, that's what I'm aimin' to do." He

laid his pipe down on the stove's fender as he resumed his recital.

"Old Proph'—which his name wasn't Prophet, of co'se, which ain't to say a name nohow, but his name was Jeremy, an' he used to go by name o' Jerry; then somebody called him Jeremy the Prophet, an' from that it got down to Prophet, and then Proph'—and so it stayed.

"Well, ez I started to say, Proph' he was jest one o' Meredith's ol' slave niggers—a sort o' queer, half-luney, no-'count darky—never done nothin' sence freedom but what he had a mind to, jest livin' on Meredith right along.

"He wasn't to say crazy, but—well, he'd stand and talk to anything—a dog, a cat, a tree, a toad-frog—*anything*. Many a time I've seen him limpin' up the road, an' he'd turn round sudden an' seemed to be talkin' to somethin' thet was follerin' him, an' when he'd git tired he'd start on an' maybe every minute look back over his shoulder an' laugh. They was only one thing Proph' was, to say, good for. Proph' was a capital A-1 hunter—shorest shot in the State, in my opinion, and when he'd take a notion he could go out where nobody wouldn't sight a bird or a squir'l all day long, an' he'd fill his game-bag.

"Well, sir, the children round town, they was all afeerd of 'im, and the niggers—th' ain't a nigger in the county thet don't b'lieve *to this day* thet Proph' would cunjer 'em ef he'd git mad.

"An' time he takin' to fortune-tellin', the school child'en thet 'd be feerd to go up to him by theirselves, they'd go in a crowd, an' he'd call out fortunes to 'em, an' they'd give him biscuits out o' their lunch-cans.

"From that time he come to tellin' anybody's fortune, an' so the young men, they got him to come to the old-year party one year, jest for the fun of it, an' time the clock was most on the twelve strike, Proph' he stood up an' called out e-vents of the comin' year. An', sir, for a crack-brained fool nigger, he'd call out the smartest things you ever hear. Every year for five year, Proph' called out comin' e-vents at the old-year party; an' matches thet nobody suspicioned, why, he'd call 'em out, an' shore enough, 'fore the year was out, the weddin's would come off. An' babies! He'd predic' babies a year ahead—not always callin' out full names, but jest insinuatin', so thet anybody thet wasn't deef in both ears would understand.

"But to come back to the story of May Meredith—he ain't in it, noways in partic'lar. It's only thet sence she could walk an' hold the ol' man's hand he doted on her, an' she was jest ez wropped up in him. Many's the time when she was a toddler he's rode into town, mule-back, with her settin' up in front of 'im. An' then when she got bigger it was jest as ef she was the queen to him—that's all. He saved her from drownd-in' once-t, jumped in the branch after her an couldn't swim a stroke, an' mos' drownded his-self—an' time she had the dip'theria, he never shet his eyes ez long ez she was sick enough to be set up with—set on the flo' by her bed all night.

"That's all the way Proph' is mixed up in her story. An' now, sence they're both gone, ef you 'magine you see one, you seem to see the other.

"But *May Day's* story? Well, I hardly like to disturb it. Don't rightly know how to tell it, nohow.

"I don't doubt folks has told you she went wrong, but that's a mighty hard way to tell it to them thet knew her.

"We can't none of us deny, I reckon, thet she went wrong. A red-cheeked peach thet don't know nothin' but the dew and the sun, and to grow sweet and purty—it goes wrong when it's wrenched off the stem and et by a hog. That's one way o' goin' wrong.

"Little Daisy Meredith didn't have no mo' idee o' harm than that mockin'-bird o' Rowton's in its cage there, thet sings week-day songs all Sunday nights.

"She wasn't but jest barely turned seventeen year—ez sweet a little girl ez ever taught a Baptist Sunday-school class—when *he* come down from St. Louis—though some says he come from Chicago, an' some says Canada—lookin' after some land mortgages. An', givin' the devil his due, he was the handsomest man thet ever trod Simpkinsville streets—that is, of co'se, for a outsider. Seen May Day first time on her way to church, an' looked after her—then squared back di-rect, an' follered her. Walked into church delib'rate, an' behaved like a gentleman religiously inclined, ef ever a well-dressed, city person behaved that way.

"Well, sir, from that day on, he froze to her, and, strange to say, every mother of a marriageable daughter in town was jealous exceptin' one, an' that one was May's own mother. An' she not only wasn't jealous—which she couldn't 'a' been, of co'se—but she wasn't pleased.

"She seemed to feel a dread of him from the start, and she treated him mighty shabby, but of co'se the little girl, she made it up to him in politeness, good ez she could, an' he didn't take no notice of it. Kep' on showin' the old lady every attention, an', when he'd be in town, most any evenin' you'd go past the Meredith gate you could see his horse hitched there—everything open and above boa'd, so it seemed.

"Well, sir, he happened to be here the time o' the old-year party, three year ago. You've been here a year and over, 'ain't you, parson?"

"Yes, I was stationed here at fall conference a year ago this November, you recollect."

"Yas, so you was. Well, all this is about two year befo' you come.

"Well, sir, when it was known thet May Day's city beau was goin' to be here for the party, everybody looked to see some fun, 'cause they knowed how free ol' Proph' made with comin' e-vents, an' they wondered ef he'd have gall enough to call out May Day's name with the city feller's. Well, ez luck would have it, the party was at my house that year, an' I tell you, sir, folks thet hadn't set up to see the old year out for ten year come that night, jest for fear they'd miss somethin'. But of co'se we saw through it. We knowed what fetched 'em.

"Well, sir, that was the purtiest party I ever see in my life. Our Simpkinsville pattern for young girls is a toler'ble neat one, ef I do say it ez shouldn't, bein' kin to forty-'leven of 'em. We 'ain't got no, to say, ugly girls in town—never had many, though some has plained down some when they got settled in years; but the girls there that night was ez perfec' a bunch of girls ez you ever see—jest ez purty a show o' beauty ez any rose arbor could turn out on a spring day.

"Have you ever went to gether roses, parson, each one seemin' to be the purtiest tell you'd got a handful, an' you'd be startin' to come away, when 'way up on top o' the vine you'd see one thet was enough pinker an' sweeter 'n the rest to make you climb for it, an' when you'd git it, you'd stick it in the top of yore bo'quet a little higher 'n the others?

"I see you know what I mean. Well, that was the way May Day looked that night. She was that top bud.

"I had three nieces, and wife she had sev'al cousins, there—all purty enough to draw hummin'-birds; but I say little Daisy Meredith, she jest topped 'em all for beauty and sweetness an' modesty that night.

"An' the stranger—well, I don't hardly know jest what to liken him to, less'n it is to one of them princes thet stalk around the stage an' give orders when they have play-actin' in a show-tent.

"They wasn't no flies on his shape, nor his rig, nor his manners neither. Talked to the old ladies—ricollect my wife she had a finger wropped up, an' he ast her about it and advised her to look after it an' give her a recipe for bone-felon. She thought they wasn't nobody like him. An' he jest simply danced the wall-flowers dizzy, give the fiddlers money, an'—well, he done everything thet a person o' the royal family of city gentry might be expected to do. An' everybody wondered what mo' Mis' Meredith wanted for her daughter. Tell the truth, some mistrusted, an' 'lowed thet she jest took on indifferent, the way she done, to hide how tickled she was over it.

"Well, ez I say, the party passed off lovely, an' after a while it come near twelve o'clock, an' the folks commenced to look round for ol' Proph' to come in an' call out e-vents same as he always done.

"So d'rectly the boys they stepped out an' fetched him in—drawin' him 'long by the sleeve, an' he holdin' back like ez ef he dreaded to come in.

"I tell you, parson, I'll never forgit the way that old nigger looked, longest day I live. Seemed like he couldn't sca'cely walk, an' he stumbled, an' when he taken his station front o' the mantel-shelf, look like he never would open his mouth to begin.

"An' when at last he started to talk, stid o' runnin' on an' laughin' an' pleggin' everybody like he always done, he lifted up his face an' raised up his hands, same ez you'd do ef you was startin' to lead in public prayer. An' then he commenced:

"Says he—an' when he started he spoke so low down in his th'oat you couldn't sca'cely hear him—says he:

"'Every year, my friends, I stands befo' you an' look throo de open gate into the new year. An',' says he, 'seem like I see a long percession o' people pass befo' me—some two-by-two, some one-by-one; some horseback, some muleback, some afoot; some cryin', some laughin'; some stumblin' ez they'd walk, an' gittin' up agin, some fallin' to rise no mo'; some faces I know, some strangers.'

"An' right here, parson, he left off for a minute, an' then when he commenced again, he dropped his voice clair down into his th'oat, an' he squinted his eyes an' seemed to be tryin' to see somethin' way off like, an' he says, says he:

"'But to-night,' says he, 'I don't know whar the trouble is,' says he, 'but, look hard ez I can, I don't seem to see clair, 'cause the sky is darkened,' says he, 'an' while I see people comin' an' goin', an' I see the doctor's buggy on the road, an' hear the church bell, an' the organ, I can't make out nothin' clair, 'cause the sky is over-shaddered by a big dark cloud. ' An' now,' says he, 'seem like the cloud is takin' the shape of a great big bird. Now I see him spread his wings an' fly into Simpkinsville, an' while he hangs over it befo' the sun seem to me I can see everybody stop an' gaze up an' hold their breath to see where he'll light—everybody hopin' to see him light in their tree. An' now—oh! now I see him comin' down, down, down—an' now he's done lit,' says he. I ricollect that expression o' his—'he's done lit,' says he, 'in the limb of a tall maginolia-tree a little piece out o' town.'

"Well, sir, when he come to the bird lightin' in a maginolia tree, a little piece out o' town, I tell you, parson, you could 'a' heerd a pin drop. You see, maginolias is purty sca'ce in Simpkinsville. Plenty o' them growin' round the edge o' the woods, but 'ceptin' them thet Sonny Simkins set out in his yard years ago, I don't know of any nearer than Meredith's place. An' right at his gate, ef you ever taken notice, there's a maginolia-tree purty nigh ez tall ez a post oak.

"An' so when the ol' nigger got to where the fine bird lit in the maginolia-tree, all them thet had the best manners, they set still, but sech ez didn't keer—an' I was one of that las' sort—why, we jest glanced at the city feller di-rec' to see how he was takin' it.

"But, sir, it didn't ruffle one of his feathers, not a one.

"An' then the nigger he went on: Says he, squintin' his eyes ag'in, an' seemin' to strain his sight, says he:

"'Now he's lit,' says he—I wish I could give it to you in his language, but I never could talk nigger talk—'now he's lit,' says he, 'an' I got a good chance to study him,' says he. 'I see he ain't the same bird he looked to be, befo' he lit.

"'His wing feathers is mighty fine, an' they rise in mighty biggoty plumes, but they can't hide his claws,' says he, 'an' when I look close-ter,' says he, 'I see he's got owl eyes an' a sharp beak, but seem like nobody can't see 'em. They all so dazzled with his wing-feathers they can't see his claws.

"'An' now whiles I'm a-lookin' I see him rise up an' fly three times round the tree, an' now I see him swoop down right befo' the people's eyes, an' befo' they know it he's riz up in the air ag'in, an' spread his wings, an' the sky seems so darkened thet I can't see nothin' clair only a long stream o' yaller hair floatin' behind him.

"'Now I see everybody's heads drop, an' I hear 'em cryin'; but,' says he, 'they ain't cryin' about the thief bird, but they cryin' about the yaller hair—the yaller hair—the yaller hair.' "

McMonigle choked a little in his recital, and then he added: "Ain't that about yore riccollection o' how he expressed it?"

"Yas," said old man Taylor, "he said it three times—I riccollect that ez long ez I live; an' the third time he said 'the yaller hair' he let his arms drop down at his side, an' he sort o' staggered back'ards, an' turned round to Johnnie Burk an' says he: 'Help me out, please, sir, I feels dizzy.' Do you riccollect how he said that, Dan'l?

"But you're tellin' the story. Don't lemme interrupt you."

"No interruption, Pete. You go on an' tell it the way you call it up. I see my pipe has done gone out while I've been talkin'. Tell the truth, I'm most sorry thet you all started me on this story to-night. It gives me a spell o' the blues—talkin' it over.

"Pass me them tongs back here, doctor, an' lemme git another coal for my pipe. An' while I've got 'em I'll shake up this fire a little. This stove's ez dull-eyed and pouty ez any other woman ef she's neglected.

"Hungry, too, ain't you, old lady? Don't like wet wood, neither. Sets her teeth on edge.

Jest listen at her quar'l while I lay it in her mouth.

"Go on, now, Pete, an' tell the parson the rest o' the story. 'Tain't no more'n right thet a shepherd should know all the ins and outs of his flock ef he's goin' to take care o' their needs."

"You better finish it, Dan'l," said Taylor. "You've brought it all back a heap better 'n I could 'a' done it."

"Tell the truth, boys, I've got it down to where I hate to go on," replied McMonigle, with feeling. "I've talked about the child now till I can seem to see her little slim figur' comin' down the plank-walk the way I've seen her a thousand times, when all the fellers settin' out in front o' the sto'es would slip in an' get their coats on, an' come back—I've done it myself, an' me a grandfather.

"Go on, Pete, an' finish it up. I've got the taste o' tobacco smoke now, an' my pipe is like the stove. Ef I neglect her she pouts.

"I left off where ol' Proph' finished prophesyin' at the old-year party at my house three year ago. I forgot to tell you, parson, thet Mis' Meredith, she never come to the party—an' Meredith hisself he only come and stayed a few minutes, an' went home 'count o' the ol' lady bein' by herself—so they wasn't neither one there when the nigger spoke. An' ef they've ever been told what he said I don't know—though we've got a half dozen smarties in town thet would 'a' busted long ago ef they hadn't 'a' told it I don't doubt.

"Go on, now, Pete, an' finish. After Proph' had got done talkin' of co'se hand-shakin' commenced, an' everybody was supposed to shake hands with everybody else. I reckon parson there knows about that—but you might tell it anyhow."

"Of co'se, parson he knows about the hand-shakin'," Taylor took up the story now, "because you was here last year, parson. You know thet it's the custom in Simpkinsville, at the old-year party, for everybody to shake hands at twelve o'clock at the comin' in of the new year. It's been our custom time out o' mind. Folks thet 'll have some fallin' out, an' maybe not be speakin', 'll come forward an' shake hands an' make up—start the new year with a clean slate.

"Why, ef 'twasn't for that, I don' know what we'd do. Some of our folks is so techy an' high strung—an' so many of 'em kin, which makes it that much worse—thet ef 'twasn't for the new-year hand-shakin', why, in a few years we'd be ez bad ez a deef and dumb asylum.

"But to tell the story. I declare, Dan'l, I

ain't no hand to tell a thing so ez to bring it befo' yo' eyes like you can. I'm feerd you'll have to carry it on."

And so old man McMonigle, after affectionately drawing a few puffs from his pipe, laid it on the fender before him, and reluctantly took up the tale.

"Well," he began, "I reckon thet rightly speakin' this is about the end of the first chapter.

"The hand-shakin' passed off friendly enough, everybody j'inin' in, though there was women thet 'lowed thet they had the cold shivers when they shuck the city feller's hand, half expectin' to tackle a bird-claw. An' I know thet wife an' me—although, understand, parson, we none o' us suspicioned no harm—we was glad when the party broke up an' everybody was gone—the nigger's words seemed to ring in our ears so.

"Well, sir, the second chapter o' the story I reckon it could be told in half a dozen words, though I s'pose it holds misery enough to make a book.

"I never would read a book thet didn't end right; in fact, I don't think the law ought to allow sech to be printed. We get enough wrong endin's in life, an' the only good book-makin' is, in my opinion, to ketch up all sech stories an' work 'em over.

"Ef I could set down an' tell May Day Meredith's story to some book-writer thet 'd take it up where I leave off, an' bring her back to us—she could even be raised from the dead *in a book* ef need be—my Lord! how I'd love to read it, an' try to b'lieve it was true! I'd like him to work the ol' nigger in at the end, too, ef he didn't think hisself above it. A ol', harmless, half-crazy nigger, thet's been movin' round amongst us all for years, is ez much missed ez anybody else when he drops out, nobody knows how. I miss Proph' jest the same ez I miss that ol' struck-by-lightnin' sycamo'-tree thet Jedge Towns has had cut out of the co't-house yard. My mother had my gran'pa's picture framed out o' sycamo' balls, gethered out of that tree forty year ago.

"But you see I'm makin' every excuse to keep from goin' on with the story, an' ef it's got to be told, well—

"Whether somebody told the Meredith's about the nigger's prophecy, an' they got excited over it, an' forbid the city feller the house, I don't know, but he never was seen goin' there after that night, though he stayed in town right along for two weeks, at the end of which time he disappeared from the face o' the earth—an' she along with him.

"An' that's all the story, parson. That's three year ago lackin' two weeks, an' nobody 'ain't seen or heard o' May Day Meredith from that day to this.

"Of co'se girls have run away with men, an' it turned out all right—but they wasn't married men. Nobody s'picioned he was married tell it was all over an' Harry Conway he heard it in St. Louis, an' it's been found to be true. An' there's a man living in Texarkana thet testified thet he was called in to witness what he b'lieved to be a genn*ine* weddin', where the preacher claimed to come from Little Rock, an' he married May Day to that man, standin' in the blue cashmere dress she run away in. She was married by the 'Piscopal prayer-book, too, which is the only thing I felt real hard against May Day for consentin' to—she being well raised, a hard-shell Baptist.

"But o' co'se the man thet could git a girl to run away with him could easy get her to change her religion."

"Hold up there, Dan'l!" interrupted old man Taylor. "Hold on, there! Not always! It's a good many years sence my ol' woman run away to marry me, but she was a Methodist, an' Methodist she's turned me, though I've been dipped, thank God!"

"Well, of co'se, there's exceptions. An' I didn't compare you to the man I'm a-talkin' about, nohow. Besides, Methodist an' 'Piscopal are two different things," returned McMonigle.

"But, tellin' my story—or at least sence I've done told the story, I'll tell parson all I know about the old nigger, Proph', which is mighty little.

"It was jest three days after May Meredith run away thet I was ridin' through the woods twixt here an' Clay Bank, an' who did I run against but old Proph'—walkin' along in the brush talkin' to hisself ez usual.

"Well, sir, I stopped my horse, an' called him up an' talked to him, an' tried to draw him out—ast him how come he to prophesy the way he done, an' how he knowed what was comin', but, sir, I couldn't get no satisfaction out of him—not a bit. He 'lowed thet he only spoke ez it was given him to speak, an' the only thing he seemed interested in was the stranger's name, an' he ast me to say it for him over and over—he repeatin' it after me. An' then he ast me to write it for him, an' he put the paper I wrote it on in his hat. He didn't know B from a bull's foot, but I s'pose he thought maybe if he put it in his hat it might strike in."

"Like ez not he 'lowed he could git somebody to read it out to him," suggested the doctor.

"Like ez not. Well, sir, after I had give him the paper he commenced to talk about huntin'—had a bunch o' birds in his hands then, an' give 'em to me, 'lowin' all the time he hadn't had much luck lately, 'count o' his pistol bein' sort o' out o' order. 'Lowed thet he took sech a notion to hunt with his pistol thet 'twasn't no fun shootin' at long range, but somehow he couldn't depend on his pistol shootin' straight.

"Took it out o' his pocket while he was standin' there, an' commenced showin' it to me. An', sir, would you believe it, while we was talkin' he give a quick turn, fired all on a sudden up into a tree, an' befo' I could git my breath, down dropped a squir'l right at his feet. Never see sech shootin' in my life. An' he wasn't no mo' excited over it than nothin'. Jest picked up the squir'l ez unconcerned ez you please, an', sez he, 'Yas, she done it that time—*but she don't always do it.* Can't depend on her.'

"Then, somehow, he brought it round to ask me ef I wouldn't loand him my revolver—jest to try it an' see if he wouldn't have better luck. 'Lowed that he'd fetch it back quick ez he got done with it.

"Well, sir, o' co'se I loaned it to the ol' nigger

—an' took his pistol—then an' there. I give it to him loaded, all six barrels, an', sir, would you believe it, no livin' soul has ever laid eyes on ol' Prophet from that day to this.

"I'm mighty feered he's wandered way off som'ers an' shot hisself accidental'—an' never was found. Them revolvers is mighty resky weepons ef a person ain't got experience with 'em.

"So that's all the story, parson. Three days after May Day went he disappeared, an' of co'se he a-livin' along at Meredith's all these years, an' being so 'tached to May Day, and prophesying about her like he done, you can see how one name brings up another. So when I think about her I seem to see him."

"Didn't Harry Conway say he see the ol' man in St. Louis once-t, an' thet he let on he didn't know him—wouldn't answer when he called him Proph'?" said old man Conway.

"One o' Harry's cock-an'-bull stories," answered McMonigle. "He might o' saw some ol' nigger o' Proph's build, but how would he git to St. Louis? Anybody's common-sense would tell him better 'n that. No, he's dead—no doubt about it."

"I suppose no one has ever looked for the old man?" the parson asked.

"Oh yas, he's been searched for. We've got up two parties an' rode out clair into the swamp lands twice-t—but there wasn't no sign of him.

"But May Day—nobody has ever went after her, of co'se. She left purty well escorted, an' ef her own folks never follered her, 'twasn't nobody else's business. Her mother 'ain't never mentioned her name sence she left—to nobody."

"Yas," interrupted the doctor, "an' some has accused her o' hard-heartedness; but when I see a woman's head turn from black to white in three months' time, like hers done, I don't say her heart's hard, I say it's broke.

"They keep a-sendin' for me to come to see her, but I can't do her no good. She's failed tur'ble last six months.

"Ef somethin' could jest come upon her sudden, to rouse her up—ef the house would burn down, an' she have to go out 'mongst other folks—or ef they was some way to git folks there, whether she wanted 'em or not—

"Tell the truth, I've been a-thinkin' about somethin'. It's been on my mind all day. I don't know ez it would do, but I been a-thinkin' ef I could get Meredith's consent for the Simpkinsville folks to come out in a body—

"Ef he'd allow it, an' the folks would be willin' to go out there to-night for the old-year party

—take their fiddle an' cakes an' things along, an' surprise her—she'd be obliged to be polite to 'em; she couldn't refuse to meet all her ol' friends for the midnight hand-shakin', an' it might be the savin' of her. Three years has passed. There's no reason why one trouble should bring another. We've all had our share o' trials this year, an' I reckon every one o' us here has paid for a tombstone in three years, an' I believe ef we'd all meet together an' go in a body out there—

"Ef you say so, I'll ride out an' talk it over with Meredith. What's your opinion, parson?"

"My folks will join you heartily, I'm sure," replied the parson, warmly. "They did expect to have the crowd over at Bradfield's to-night, but I know they'll be ready to give in to the Meredith's."

And this is how it came about that the Meredith's house, closed for three years, opened its doors again.

If innocent curiosity and love of fun had carried many to the new-year hand-shaking three years before, a more serious interest, not unmixed with curiosity, swelled the party to-night.

It was a mile out of town. The night was

stormy, the roads were heavy, and most of the wagons without cover; but the festive spirit is impervious to weather the world over, and there were umbrellas in Simpkinsville, and overcoats and "tarpaulins."

Everybody went. Even certain good people who had not previously been able to master their personal animosities sufficiently to resolve to present themselves for the midnight hand-shaking, and had decided to nurse their grievances for another year, now promptly agreed to bury their little hatchets and join the party.

To storm a citadel of sorrow, whether the issue should prove a victory for besiegers or besieged, was no slight lure to a people whose excitements were few, and whose interests were limited to the personal happenings of their small community.

It is a crime in the provincial code-social to excuse one's self from a guest. To deny a full and cordial reception to all the town would be to ostracise one's self forever, not only from its society, but from all its sympathies.

The weak-hearted hostess rallied all her failing energies for the emergency. And there was no lack of friendliness in her pale old face as she greeted her most unwelcome guests with extended timorous hands.

If her thin cheeks flushed faintly as her neighbors' happy daughters passed before her in game or dance, her solicitous observers, not suspecting the pain at her heart, whispered: "Mis' Meredith is chirpin' up a'ready. She looks a heap better 'n when we come in." So little did they understand.

If mirth and numbers be a test, the old-year party at the Merediths' was assuredly a success.

Human emotions swing as pendulums from tears to laughter. Those of the guests to-night who had declared that they knew they would burst out crying as soon as they entered that house where the ones who laughed the loudest.

"Spinning the plate," "dumb-crambo," "pillow," "how, when and where," such were the innocent games that composed the simple diversions of the evening, varied by music by the village string-band and occasional songs from the girls, all to end with a "Virginia. break-down" just before twelve o'clock, when the handshaking should begin.

It seemed a very merry party, and yet, in speaking of it afterwards, there were many who declared that it was the saddest evening they had ever spent in their lives, some even affirming that they had been "obliged to set up an' giggle the live-long time to keep from cryin' every time they looked at Mis' Meredith."

Whether this were true, or only seemed to be true in the light of subsequent events, it would be hard to say. Certain it was, however, that the note that rose above the storm and floated out into the night was one of joyous merrymaking. Such was the note that greeted a certain slowly moving wagon, whose heavily clogged wheels turned into the Merediths' gate near midnight. The belated guest was evidently one entirely familiar with the premises, for notwithstanding the darkness of the night, the ponderous wheels turned accurately into the curve beyond the magnolia-tree, moved slowly but surely along the drive up to the door, and stopped without hesitation exactly opposite the "landing at the front stoop," wellnigh invisible in the darkness.

After the ending of the final dance, during the very last moments of the closing year, there was always at the old-year party an interval of silence.

The old men held their watches in their hands, and the young people spoke in whispers.

It was this last waiting interval that in years past the old man Prophet had filled with portent, even though, until his last prophecy, his words had been lightly spoken.

As the crowd sat waiting to-night, watching the slow hands of the old clock, listening to the never-hurrying tick-tack of the long pendulum against the wall, it is probable that memory, quickened by circumstances and environment, supplied to every mind present a picture of the old man, as he had often stood before them.

A careful turn of the front-door latch, so slight a click as to be scarcely discernible, came at this moment as the clank of a sledge-hammer, turning all heads with a common impulse towards the slowly opening door, into which limped a tall, muffled figure. To the startled eyes of the company it seemed to reach quite to the ceiling. Those sitting near the door started back in terror at the apparition, and all were on their feet in a moment.

But having entered, the figure halted just within the door, and before there was time for action, or question even, a bundle of old wraps had fallen and the old man Prophet, bearing in his arms a golden-haired cherub of about two years, stood in the presence of the company.

The revulsion of feeling, indescribable by words, was quickly told in fast-flowing tears. Looking upon the old negro and the child, everyone present read a new chapter in the home tragedy, and wept in its presence.

Coming from the dark night into the light, the old man could not for a moment discern the faces he knew, and when the little one, shrinking from the glare, hid her face in his hair, it was as if time had turned back, so perfect a restoration was the picture of a familiar one of the old days. No word had yet been spoken, and the ticking of the great clock, and the crackling of the fire mingled with sobs, were the only sounds that broke the stillness when the old man, having gotten his bearings, walked directly up to Mrs. Meredith and laid the child in her arms. Then, losing no time, but pointing to the clock that was slowly nearing the hour, he said, in a voice tremulous with emotion: "De time is most here. Is you all ready to shek hands? Ef you is—*everybody*—turn round and come wid me."

As he spoke he turned back to the still open door, and before those who followed had taken in his full meaning, he had drawn into the room a slim, shrinking figure, and little May Day Meredith, pale, frightened and weather-beaten, stood before them.

If it was her own father who was first to grasp her hand, and if he carried her in his arms to her mother, it was that the rest deferred to his first claim, and that their hearty and affectionate greetings came later in their proper order. As the striking of the great clock mingled with the sound of joy and of weeping—the congratulations and words of praise fervently uttered—it made a scene ever to be held dear in the annals of Simpkinsville. It was a scene beyond words of description—a family meeting which even lifetime friends recognized as too sacred for their eyes, and hurried weeping away.

It was when the memorable, sad, joyous party was over, and all the guests were departing, that Prophet, following old man McMonigle out, called him aside for a moment. Then putting into his hands a small object, he said, in a tremulous voice:

"Much obleeged for de loand o' de pistol, Marse Dan'l. Hold her keerful, caze she's loaded des de way you loaded her—all 'cept one barrel. I ain't nuver fired her but once-t."

WEEDS

A ROMANCE OF THE SIMPKINSVILLE CEMETERY

WEEDS

ELIJAH TOMKINS stood looking down upon his wife's grave. It was early morning, and he thought himself alone in the cemetery.

The low rays of a rising sun, piercing the intervening foliage, lay in white spots of light upon the new mound, revealing an incipient crop of rival grasses there. A heavy dew, visible everywhere in all-pervading moisture, hung in glistening gems upon the blades of bright green cocoa spears that had shot up between the drier clods, and it lay in little pools within the compact hearts of the fat purslane clumps that were settling in the lower places. But Elijah saw none of these things.

He had been standing here some minutes, his head low upon his bosom, when a slight sound startled him. It was a faint crackle, as of a light footstep upon the gravel walk.

He turned suddenly and looked behind him. He saw nothing, but the start had roused him from his reverie, and he hastily proceeded to raise his walking-cane, which he had held behind him, and to thrust it with care several inches deep into the top of the grave. Then withdrawing it, he dropped into the hole it had made a rose-bud, which he took from his pocket, drew a bit of earth over it, and hastened away.

Elijah had done precisely this thing every morning since his wife's death, three weeks ago.

There were exactly twenty-one rose-buds buried in this identical fashion, one for each day since the filling of the new grave, and most of them had been deposited there before the rising of the morning sun.

Elijah was a man to whom any display of sentiment was childish; or, what to one of his temper was perhaps even worse, it was "womanish." To "fool with flowers" in a sentimental way was, according to his thinking, as unbecoming a man as to "spout poetry" or to "play the piany."

He had passed safely through all the vicissitudes of courtship, marriage, and even a late paternity—that crucial test of mental poise—without succumbing to any of the traditional follies incident to these particular epochs. He had borne his honors simply, as became a man, without parade or apparent emotion. But with his widowerhood had come an obligation involving tremendous embarrassment.

Elijah had loved his wife, and when on her death-bed she had asked him to come every day and lay a rose-bud upon her grave he had not been able to say her nay. No one had heard the request. None knew of the promise.

On the day following the funeral he had risen early, saddled his horse, and ridden to the graveyard, carrying the rose-bud openly in his hand. He had slept heavily that night—the sleep of exhaustion that comes as a boon at such times—and when he had waked next morning, confronted suddenly by a sense of his loss and of his promise, he had set out upon his initial journey without a touch of self-consciousness. It was only when he unexpectedly came upon a neighbor in the road that he instantly knew that he was doing a sentimental thing. At the surprise the flower turned downward, falling out of sight behind the pommel of his saddle as if by its own volition. And when Elijah had passed his neighbor with a silent greeting, his horse's head turned, as if he too were denying the sentimental journey, into a foot-path leading entirely away from the cemetery.

When he had gotten quite beyond the curve of the road, it was a simple thing to turn across a bit of wood and enter the graveyard by another gate, but as he did so Elijah knew himself for a hopeless coward. The crackling pine-needles under his horse's feet sounded as thunder to his sensitive ears. Every bur seemed to turn upon him its hundred eyes, in which he saw all Simpkinsville gazing at him, a mourning widower carrying flowers. The twitterings of the wood were the whisperings of the village gossips, and some of the younger trees even giggled as he passed.

To say that the widower's grief commands scant sympathy in Simpkinsville is putting the case leniently.

Indeed, it is no uncommon thing in this otherwise kindly village for the friends who sit up with the body of a deceased wife to indulge in whispered speculations as to her probable successor, and any undue exhibition of emotion on the part of the bereaved husband is counted as presaging early consolation.

This may seem harsh, perhaps, and yet it is said that the hypothesis is amply sustained by the history of widowerhood and its repairs in these parts.

It is possible that such exhibition of feeling is

sometimes a simple revolt against the lonely life as insupportable.

It may have been so, indeed, in the most notable case in the annals of Simpkinsville, when a certain inconsolable widower of effusive habit proceeded, on the demise of his wife, whose name was Lily, to adopt a lily as his trade-mark stencilled upon his cotton-bales, to bestow the name promiscuously upon all the eligibles born upon his plantation, from a pickaninny of chocolate hue to a bay colt, and to have all flowers excepting the lilies extracted from his garden. Indeed, he even went so far as to change the name of his place from "Phœnix Farm" to "Lilyvale," and when at the end of a year of full florescence the odor of the white flower pervaded every nook and cranny of his home he suddenly succumbed to the blushing wiles of a certain "Miss Rose ——" of the country-side, and there was a changing of names and a planting of roses with some confusion.

There were jests galore about the rose's thorns scratching up the lily bulbs in this particular garden of the winged god, and the slight residuum of sympathy possible towards the mourning widower passed forever out of the popular heart with the legend of the lily and the rose.

Everybody in Simpkinsville and its environments had known and laughed at this romance of a year. Elijah had simply cleared his throat and been disgusted over it, but it will be easily seen that such a precedent might somewhat heighten the sensitiveness of so timid a man to the perils of the situation as he entered upon his daily pilgrimage.

He had not meant to bury the rose that first morning. The interment was an after-thought; but it was so simple a thing to do that he had easily seized upon it as a direct way out of his difficulty.

A man of poetic feeling might have found pleasure in the reflection that in thus personally bestowing the flower he made it more exclusively hers who lay beneath it than if the knowledge of it were shared by others. But Elijah did not go so far. His satisfaction was rather that of him who thinks he has found a way to eat his pie and have it too.

As we have seen, he had been burying his daily bud for three weeks when this recital begins, and he believed himself still unobserved. He had always been an early riser, and the cemetery was so near the road to his own fields that he found the early détour quite a safe thing. One meeting him on the road would not question his errand.

"HE HAD BEEN BURYING HIS DAILY BUD FOR THREE WEEKS"

The fright he had felt at the suspicion of footsteps in the graveyard this morning remained with him as he turned homeward. Once before he had been startled in this way, and each time the false alarm had been a warning. It had frightened him.

"Strange how women takes notions, anyhow!" he muttered, as, the sense of panic still upon him, he turned to go. This was his first confessed revolt. "Never knowed Jinny to be so awful set on rose-buds, nohow, when she was here. Not thet I'd begrudge her all the roses in creation ef she wanted 'em. But for a middle-aged couple like us to be made laughin'-stalks of jest for a few buds thet I'm doubtful ef she ever receives, it does seem—"

He had just reached this point in his soliloquy when an unmistakable creaking sound startled him, and he turned suddenly to see the vanishing edge of a woman's skirt as it disappeared behind the hedge of Confederate jasmine that enclosed the family burial lot of a certain John Christian, a year ago deceased.

He had heard, long before his own bereavement, that Christian's widow spent a great part of her time at her husband's grave, but he had heard it at a time when such things held no special interest for him, and it had passed out of his mind. But now the discovery of her actual presence here filled him with panic. It was not likely that she had seen him this morning. The Christian lot was near the other gate, by which she had evidently entered, and her back had been in his direction. But she would be coming again.

Elijah was so fearful of discovery that he dared not risk another step, and so he sat down upon a stump in the shade of a weeping-willow and waited.

The widow Christian was short, and the jasmine hedge was tall. The opening in the green enclosure, indicated by an arch of green, was upon its opposite side, so Elijah had not seen her enter it, but presently the shaking of the upper branches of the vines showed that the training hand was within the square. Once or twice a slender finger appeared above the hedge as it drew a wiry tendril into place, and there was an occasional clipping of shears as the wayward vine received further discipline from the pruning-blade within.

Long after there was any sign of her presence Elijah sat waiting for the widow to go, but still she stayed. It seemed an age, and he grew very tired, and under the pressure of imprisonment and fatigue he presently began to amuse himself with idle thoughts—thoughts about the hedge first, then about the man who lay within its enclosure, and then, by natural sequence, about his widow.

"Pore Christian!" he began. "He was hedged in purty close-t with her religion long ez he lived—an' I see she's a-follerin' it up! A reg'lar Presbyterian cut that hedge has got—a body 'd know it to look at it. A shoutin' Methodist, now, might 'a' let it th'ow out sprouts right an' left, an' give God the glory."

From this, his first idle thought, it will be seen that Elijah was a man of some imagination. May it not, indeed, have been this very imagination, with a latent sense of humor, that put so keen an edge upon his anguish in a ridiculous situation?

His shrugging shoulders gave silent expression to a repressed chuckle, as he followed his rambling thoughts still further in this wise:

"Umh! Well, I reckon she knows what she's about in keepin' a close-t watch over his grave. She's afeerd some o' them few wild-oats she never give him a chance to sow might sprout up an' give him away. Umh!"

His growing pleasure in this momentary mental emancipation seemed to shorten the period of his waiting.

"Well, ef wild-oats is ez long-lived ez what wheat is, she can't no mo'n ward off the growth du'ing her lifetime—that is, ef what parson sez is true, thet a grain o' wheat has laid in a ol' tombstone 'longside one o' these dumby mummies a thousand years, an' then sprouted quick ez it was took out. Hard to swaller, that story is, for a farmer, thet's had to do with mildewed seeds, but I reckon ef preachers don't know the ins an' outs of mummies, nobody don't. But the way I look at it, any chemicals thet's strong enough to keep a mummy in countenance that long would exercise a savin' influ'nce on anything layin' round him, maybe. Pity they couldn't be applied to a man *in life*, so ez to—Jack Robinson! What in thunder— She's a-comin' this way!"

It is a long way from the buried secrets of Egypt to the Simpkinsville cemetery, and to be transported the entire distance in a twinkling by the apparition of a dreaded woman bearing down upon one is what might be called a jolting experience. This is exactly what happened to Elijah at this trying moment.

The widow Christian had stepped briskly out of the enclosure, and was facing the tree under which he sat.

There be "weeping-willows" that truly

weep, while some, with all the outward semblance of sorrow, do seem only to whine and whimper, so sparse and attenuated are their dripping fringes—fringes capable even of flippancy if the wind be of a flirtatious mind.

Of this latter sort was the one beneath which Elijah had taken refuge this morning. The meagre ambush that had seemed quite adequate in the lesser exigency was as nothing now as through its flimsy screen he saw disaster surely approaching. But his moment of supreme panic was mercifully brief.

Before she had reached his hiding-place the widow turned hastily aside. She was bent upon a definite destination, and Elijah had scarcely had time to rally from his first fright before he discovered that she was going to his wife's grave. He could not see her when she had reached it, but he saw distinctly her lengthened shadow on the sward behind her. When at last she stopped there, he even saw this same witness make a deliberate tour of the grave. He saw it bend and rise and fall, and then, when it was gone, he watched for the widow to appear at the farther side, and he saw her at last go out the graveyard gate. In a moment more he heard the roll of wheels, and, standing up, he even descried the top of her buggy as she drove away. And then, taking off his hat and mopping his forehead, he came out of hiding.

This visit to his wife's grave gave Elijah a most uncomfortable sensation, and he hurried there to see how things were. He had, he knew, carefully covered his morning bud, but still he was uneasy.

When he returned to the grave he found the grass upon it dry. There seemed to be otherwise no change in its appearance, and he was turning away, somewhat reassured, when a fresh clod caught his eye. It seemed to have been overturned. He stooped down, his heart thumping like a sledge-hammer, while he made a careful examination.

The clod lay exactly over the spot where he had, an hour ago, deposited his rose-bud, and its damp side was upward. A bent hair-pin lay beside it, and there was damp earth upon its points. Lifting the lump, he found its nether side still warm from the sun. Beneath it, clearly discernible without further removal, was the pink edge of a rose leaf.

Elijah was not ordinarily a nervous man, but when he rose from the grave he was trembling so that he felt it safe to repair to his seat beneath the willow until he should recover himself.

The next moments were possibly as wretched

as any that had hitherto come into his life. As he sat with his face buried in his hands, he felt the same sort of exquisite torture that he had occasionally experienced in a dream, when for a brief moment he had believed himself walking the streets naked, in a glare of light, and had waked up with a start to a blessed consciousness of a friendly darkness and his night-shirt. There was no awakening possible now. A second trip to the grave only prolonged the horrors of the nightmare. He took off his hat again and mopped and mopped his face and head and neck. Then, in sheer desperation, he began walking slowly up and down the gravelled paths, his hands nervously clasped behind him, and before he realized it he found himself at the opening in the Christian hedge, and he walked in.

There was a pretty rustic seat just within the enclosure, and he sat down upon it. Even his state of mind, and the fresh impression of the obtrusive widow rudely etched with the muddy point of a hair-pin upon the sensitive plate of his consciousness, could not prevent his feeling the sweetness and beauty of this spot. The grave in its centre was already, in the early spring, a bed of blooming flowers. Tender sprays of smilax climbed about the marble slab at its head, while from the urn at the foot of the mound depended rich garlands of moneywort and tradescantia, and the air was fragrant with the perfumed leaf of pungent herb and flowering shrub.

Along the lower borders of the mound, just above a battlement of inverted bottles that outlined its extreme limits, there were signs of the recent passage of the trowel, and here closer scrutiny revealed a single line of wilting plants, evidently just set out.

Elijah looked about him for some moments, and then, man that he was, he began to cry. Perhaps it was essential to his manhood that his emotion should be interpreted as anger. At any rate, the turmoil within him found expression in words that, as nearly as they could be distinguished among sobs, were such as these:

"The idee of John Christian, thet never did a decent thing in his life, layin' comf'tably down in sech a place ez this—an' bein' waited on—an' bloomed over! An' here I, thet have tried to ac' upright all my life, am obligated to be a laughin'-stalk to his fool widder an' anybody she's a mind to tell! They've been times in my life when I'd give every doggone cent I've made du'in' my durn blame life ef I'd 'a' been raised to swear—I'll be jim-blasted ef I wouldn't! No widder of sech a low-down, beer-drinkin' cuss ez

John Christian need to think she can set out to pester *me*—a-nosin' round my private business with her confounded investigatin' hair-pin! They ain't nothin' thet a woman with a hair-pin ain't capable of doin'—nothin'!"

He sobbed for some time without further words; but presently, while he wiped his eyes, he said, in quite another voice:

"Ef—ef Jinny had jest 'a' had the fo'thought to say *bushes* instid o' *buds*, why—why, they'd 'a' been planted long ago—*an' forgot*—an' she'd be havin' her own roses fresh every day; instid o' which—" And now he sobbed again. "Instid o' which John Christian's widder has got the satisfaction of holdin' me up on a hair-pin p'int for all Simpkinsville to laugh at—same ez ef I was some sort o' guyaskutus!"

As he raised his face, dashing his tears away with his great bare hands, his eyes fell upon the inscription upon the stone before him. The Bible verse quoted there seemed an assumption of superior sanctity, and he resented it as a personal taunt.

"Yas," he retorted, "I see you're takin' to quotin' Scripture, John Christian, but you needn't to quote it at me! You're set out first class, you are, Bible tex' at yo' head an' flower-vase at yo' feet, but you ain't the first low-down cuss thet's been Bible-texted out of all recognition."

Was it the answering silence of the grave in response to this volley that rebuked him? Perhaps so, for certainly there was sudden contrition expressed in his next words, spoken in apologetic voice:

"God forgive me for strikin' a man when he's down; but he does seem so set up—flowered all over—an' nothin' to do—an' a lovin' wife—"

Just as Elijah said these last words there was a stir at his side, and he turned to see the widow Christian standing before him, plants and trowel in hand. She started on first perceiving him, but his tearful, dejected state was an appeal to her womanly sympathies. She took her seat beside him on the settee.

"Yas," she said, mournfully, "everybody knows she was a lovin' wife, Mr. Tomkins, an' I ain't surprised to see you all broke up this way. I been through it all, an' I know what it is." She sighed heavily. "They ain't a grain o' the bitterness but I've tasted—not a one—an' quinine an' bitter alloways is sugar to it. But I'm mighty glad, Mr. Tomkins, to see thet you feel neighborly enough to come into my lot to give way. You'll be all the better for it. It's what I do myself. When I git nervous in the house, an' seem to look for *him* to come in, an' feel sort o' like ez ef he might be down-town an' maybe things goin' wrong, why, I jest come here, an' I see it's all right, an' I cry it out an' go home.

"I hate to see you come twice-t in one day, though, Mr. Tomkins," she added, after some hesitation. "*Too much* sorrer starts the heart a-cankerin'! Somehow I had a notion thet you'd been here an' gone over a hour ago. I come an' set out this row o' pansies round the edge of his grave befo' sunup—an' I was jest seven short. So I went an' fetched these to finish the line."

To attempt to describe Elijah's sensations during these first moments would be folly. He simply had none. It was a season of general suspensions.

In speaking of it afterwards, he said: "While she set there a-talkin', seem like she'd move away off into the distance tell she wasn't no bigger 'n a chiney doll, an' every word she'd say would sound clair an' fine same ez ef a doll-baby was to commence to talk by machinery. An' when she'd be away off an' dwindlin' down to a speck, I'd be gittin' bigger an' bigger tell I'd seem like a sort o' swole-up pin-cushion with needles a-stickin' in me all over. Then she'd start forward an' commence to git bigger, an'

I'd swivel an' swivel, tell time she come up to me, with a voice like thunder, I'd be so puny seem like I was li'ble to go out any minute."

But in this view of the situation we have the advantage of the retrospect.

The visible picture at the time was of Tomkins politely facing his entertainer, with possibly too much solicitude as to the wiping of his face, but still with what she was pleased to accept as polite attention. She could have suspected nothing abnormal in it, for her next words were:

"But I ain't a-goin' to bother you now, Mr. Tomkins; you jest take yo' time to ease up, an' I'll plant these plants. They go in right here at his feet."

Even as she spoke she fell upon her knees and set about her task. But there was no intermission in her talk.

"You don't know what a comfort this grave is to me, Mr. Tomkins," she said, with a sigh, as, taking a pin from her back hair, she began carefully drawing out the damp roots of the plant she held. "Ef a body studies over it rightly, there's a heap o' communion with the dead th'ough grave-tendin'! Now these pansies here —f'instance— Pansies, you know—why, they're flowers of remembrance, an' a person can plant any kind they see fit, accordin' to their hearts' desires. There's the yallers and deep reds—an' mixed. Some o' the mixed ones is marked so ez to make reg'lar fool faces. These here are all dead black." She sighed again. "I did think I'd put in a purple or two this season, but I 'ain't had the heart to—not yet. He hated black," she added in a moment, "but of co'se in this *my* heart has to have *some* consideration, an' I've done a good many things to pacify him—

"These bottles, f'instance—" She sat back upon her heels, while her eye made the circuit of the bottle border. "These bottles, now," she repeated, with manifest hesitation—"I 'ain't never mentioned them to nobody before, Mr. Tomkins, an' I don't know why I'm a-doin' it to you, 'less 'n it's seein' you in the same state o' mind thet I've been th'ough. You'll find, ez you go on, Mr. Tomkins, thet unless a heart gets expressed one way or another, its mighty ap' to palpitate inwardly. Have you ever had yo' heart to palpitate inward, Mr. Tomkins?"

She had turned, and was looking straight into her guest's face. He had had time to begin to recover his bearings by this time. The *me* and the *not me* were gradually assuming proper relations in his returning consciousness. To be exact, he had just begun definitely to realize where he sat, and that John Christian's widow was talking to him when she put her question.

His first conscious act had been to stop mopping his face and to put his handkerchief away. It was while he was in the act of this bestowal that there came a realization of her expectant face and the necessity of speech.

"Well, reely—Mis' Christian—" he began.

"Of co'se," she interrupted, "you may've had it an' not known it. You tell it by feelin' the need of somethin' an' not knowin' jest what it is. It might be fresh air or aromatic sperits of ammonia, an' then again it might be somebody to talk to. With some it's religion. Of co'se, with me—with me it's been this grave.

"These bottles, now—ef they was one thing on earth thet could 'a' been called a bone of contention in our lives, Mr. Tomkins, it was them identical bottles. I don't reckon I'm a-tellin' you any secret when I say that. Everybody was obligated to know pore John's one fault, because it was that sort of a fault—outspoke an' confessed. That's where John was unlucky. They's lots o' folks thet passes for better 'n what he passed thet has inward faults thet he'd 'a' spewed out o' his mouth. Sech ez that I class ez whited sepulchures—nothin' else. But his one outward fault—why, someway it nagged me constant, an' I know I never showed proper patience with it.

"But now"—she sighed sadly—"but now I've took every endurin' bottle I could lay hands on thet he ever emptied, an' I've brought 'em to him here. An' I've laid my pansy line 'longside of 'em. But I can't say yet thet they ain't a thorn in the flesh to me sometimes—them bottles.

"An' I've even done more than that, Mr. Tomkins; I've planted mint here—jest ez a token of forgiveness—nothin' else. An', tell the truth, I'm even gittin' so's I like the smell of it. May-be I'll git entirely reconciled to the bottles—in time. I've had mighty little patience with spear-mint all these years, which I now reelize was very foolish, 'cause a green herb ain't no ways respon-sible for the company it's made to keep, an' I don't know ez they's anything thet could take the mint's place in a julep an' do less harm 'n what the mint does. I don't know but it's may-be a savin' grace to it; an' then it's a Bible herb, you know—mint an' anise an' cumin."

She had turned away now, and was resuming her work of transplanting. Her last words were spoken as if in half-forgetfulness of her guest. Still, this was possibly only in the seeming, for she said, in a moment, "This is every bit a work of love, Mr. Tomkins." She dropped a pansy into place as she spoke, measuring its distance from the inverted bottle with the length of her hair-pin. "He always said he didn't want no foolishness made over his grave — but I think sech modesty ez that should have its reward."

She had presently completed her planting, and after she had scraped the trowel with her hair-pin, cleansed the pin's point in turn against the blade, and then wiped them upon a folded leaf, she mechanically restored the little implement to her hair and rose from her knees.

"I'm reel glad I had to come back to finish that transplantin', ez it's turned out, Mr. Tomkins." She looked straight at him, with absolute ingenuousness, as she spoke. "I'm glad, 'cause I feel thet I've been able to offer you a *little* consolation. I was tempted to let them plants lay over tell to-morrer, but I thought I'd feel mo' contented all day ef every beer-bottle had its pansy. Ef they was anything over, I'd ruther it would be a pansy, to make shore of lovin' forgiveness."

She had turned again to the grave now.

"I don't often count my plants when I fetch 'em over, an' I mos' gen'ally have a few to spare, an' I set 'em round on graves thet don't have much care. I try to keep the potter's field a-bloomin' a little with my left-overs."

She had taken her seat at Tomkins's side again and laid the trowel in her lap. Her bonnet-strings needed retying, and there was a suspicion of dust to be brushed from her knees.

"I did carry a handful of left-over flowers around to plant on pore Crazy Charlie's grave one day, but when I got there I found thet the Lord had took care o' the pore idiot's memory better'n I could 'a' done. It was all broke out thick ez measles with dandelions, an' sez I to myself, ef they ever was a flighty flower on the green earth, it's a dandelion. So I come away an' planted my odds an' ends promiscuous. I've often wondered ef dandelions wasn't reckoned ez idiots among flowers."

It was no doubt an awful thing for Elijah to do, certainly it was most inconsistent with his position as taken seriously from any point of view, but at this juncture he suddenly surrendered himself to uncontrollable laughter.

After a first startled glance his entertainer smiled.

"Well, I declare!" She spoke kindly. "I've done a good mornin's work, Mr. Tomkins, ef it's only to give you a good, hearty laugh. You'll be all the better for it."

It is one thing to laugh, and quite another not to be able to stop laughing. Tomkins was for some minutes precisely in this condition. He was so overcome, indeed, that he finally turned his back, and, burying his face in his handkerchief, shook until the bench rattled.

Fortunately his hostess was a woman of genial humor, and, as she has amply shown, by no means a person of sensitiveness.

"You'll likely cry a little again when the laugh's over—I always do—but it's jest that much better for you," she said, cheerily, as she rose to go. "And now, *good*-bye!"

As she moved away, Tomkins suddenly realized something that sobered him. She must *not* go until there should be some understanding about his buried rose-buds. If possible, he must have her promise of secrecy.

There was a sudden pain in his heart and a sense of shame as the tender subject presented itself anew to his mental vision. His sorrow was fresh and sacred. The woman with whom he must temporize had invaded its holy domain, and he felt, even as he hastened to pursue her, that he despised her.

She was a lithe little woman, of quick step, and by the time Elijah had disposed of his troublesome emotions sufficiently to present himself he saw that she was nearing the gate, and he called her, faintly:

"Oh, Mis' Christian!"

She immediately turned and started back.

"Nemmind; don't come back; I jest want to talk to you a little bit."

He overtook her now, and together they proceeded to the gate.

"Mis' Christian, I've jest been a-thinkin'," he began—"that is, I've been a-wonderin'—I wonder ef you're the kind o' person—I know you're a mighty nice lady, Mis' Christian, an' a tender-hearted one, which you've showed me today, unmistakable—but I was jest a-wonderin' ef you was the kind o' person"—they had reached the gate now, and Elijah leaned against the post, hesitating in awkward embarrassment—"ef you was the sort o' person thet, ef you was to know a little thing about another person thet they was a-tryin' to keep hid—for reasons of their own—would you jest keep it to yo'self, please, ma'am, an' not say nothin' about it? I'd like to think you *was* that kind o' person, Mis' Christian—I would indeed."

A great, pleased light came into the widow's eyes. They saw the dawn of a new era in this interesting case, and this was its reflection. She mechanically loosened her bonnet strings as she came nearer to Elijah.

"Mr. Tomkins," she began, seriously, and

with evident relish, "I'm mighty glad you've spoke. Of co'se yo' silence wasn't a thing for me to break. A person's silence is his own—to break or to keep—an' you've broke yores an' let me in—an' I come ez a friend. But befo' I go a step further, Mr. Tomkins"—she came nearer now and lowered her voice—"befo' I go a step further, I want to tell you roses don't grow by plantin' buds. They have to be set out in cuttin's. You could come here an' plant rose-buds all yo' mortal life, an' you wouldn't never have so much ez a sprout, much less 'n a rose-bush—not ef you planted tell doomsday."

Elijah blushed scarlet. "An' *do* you think, Mis' Christian, thet—"

"I don't *think* nothin' about it. I *know* it. But ez for *talkin'!* Why, horses an' mules couldn't drag a word out o' me about yo' plantin' them buds. I been wantin' to tell you for three weeks thet you wouldn't have no crop, but, ez I said befo', it wasn't for me to break yore silence. I wanted to tell you partly on *her* account, too, 'cause ef she's conscious of it, I know it must pleg her. She was so sensible always, I know how she'd feel."

Elijah moved uneasily, shifting his weight from one foot to the other.

"Mis' Christian," he began, "we're here in

the presence o' the dead, ez you might say, an' I'm a-goin' to talk to you outspoke. My feelin's ain't things I like to talk about—an' I'm a slow-spoken man anyway. Either my luck or yores is the lot of purty nigh every married couple in God's world. Mighty few is allotted to die together. They's bound to be a *goer* an' a *stayer,* an' ef the goers can stand their part an' keep silence, it's always seemed to me the stayers might do ez much—jest hold still—that's all. I thought I was man enough to do it—an' *I am* ef—" He wanted to say "ef I could be let alone," but he dared not. He left the sentence broken. "But ef they's one thing on the round world thet *I can't* stand, it's bein' made a fool of—or laughed at. An' that's why I planted them buds."

The widow looked at him askance, as if half suspicious of his sanity. But he went on:

"*She* ast me, Mis' Christian—one o' the last words she spoke—*an' I promised her*—to put a rose-bud on her grave every day—an' I've done it. But I knowed thet ef I was *ketched* a-doin' sech a softy thing, they wouldn't be no peace in Simpkinsville for me—so I've jest buried it. An' continue to do so I must.

"Now I've done out with the whole thing. It seemed like a little thing to ask. Buds is plentiful, an' the cemetery is close-t enough, an' I'd do a'most anything to please her. An' yet— Well, it's jest one o' them little things sech ez a woman 'll ask a man to do *in a minute*, an' he'll *never git done doin'*. Th' ain't *nothin'* I wouldn't do for her, *an' do gladly*, thet I could *keep to myself*. Ef she'd 'a' ast me to eat a whole rose-bush every day, I'd eat it gladly, thorns an' all. They'd be a-plenty o' ways of eatin' it in secret, an' I wouldn't mind a inward thorn. But this here trip I'm obligated to take—tell the truth, it plegs me. An' now, I don't doubt thet to a woman with sech a bloomin' grave ez you keep I must seem like a mighty begrudgin' sort of a man, Mis' Christian."

"Not at all, Mr. Tomkins—not at all. You're jest precizely, for all the world, similar-dispositioned to John Christian. Ef I had 'a' died first, although he'd 'a' been all broke up over it, I know I wouldn't have no mo' flowers on my grave than sech weeds ez the good Lord sends to beggars' graves—not a one. Pore John! He often said, jest a-jokin', of co'se, thet he'd promise thet I should wear weeds, no matter which went first. He was death on jokin' that-a-way. Little did he think I'd wear both kinds, though, pore John, which no doubt I will. They won't be nobody but God to flower me over when I'm gone. I've often thought I'd like to get in under 'em—when my time comes—and enjoy my own flowers awhile. His grave is a-plenty wide. But of co'se they wouldn't be no way of gettin' me in without upsettin' things, an' I reckon it's jest ez well. Ef I knew the flowers was there I'd have 'em on my mind all the time, an' every dry spell I'd be fidgety to get out an' water 'em. In tendin' his grave, Mr. Tomkins, I take the same pleasure I would 'a' took ef I *was* in it an' *he* fixin' it up. Doin' ez you'd be done by is sometimes mo' satisfyin' than bein' *did* by. 'Cause them thet do by you don't always come up to the mark.

"But don't think I blame you, Mr. Tomkins. Where they's one person foreordained to carry rose-buds around, there's been a hundred foreordained to laugh at him.

"But it looks to me like ez if we ought to be able to devise some way to have you relieved. Of co'se you've got to keep on—ez long ez rose-buds hold out. An' of co'se they's a long summer ahead, an' buds 'll be plentiful, but the last two winters have been so mild thet they's a big freeze prophesied next year. An' ef buds give out, ez they're more'n likely to, why, it won't be yo' fault. An' ef she sees into yo' heart she'll see thet it warms so to desher the day the roses freeze thet she wouldn't be indoooced to have you start it another season. An' don't you fret. Jest go along plantin' yore buds, an' nobody livin' but you an' me an' this gate-post 'll ever know it.

"An' any time you feel the need of givin' way, jest come over to his square an' make yo'self at home, whether I'm there or not. We all have our trials, Mr. Tomkins, an' when yore buds seem mo' than you can bear, why jest remember thet I've got my beer-bottles. *Good*-bye!"

She held out her hand. Tomkins took it heartily, without a word, and then, turning away, he proceeded to unfasten her horse, and to turn him while she jumped into her buggy.

As he handed her the reins, lifting his hat as he did so, he was startled by the sound of approaching wheels.

Involuntarily at the sound he dodged into the open gate and hurried back through the cemetery to his horse, tied at the other gate. And even in his hurry and fright, as he strode rapidly through the winding paths, this comforting thought took shape and soothed his troubled mind:

"'Stonishin' what a sensible woman Christian's wife is, after all!"

She was to him quite as truly the dead man's wife as if her lamented husband were still living.

Her friendly interest and sympathy had been that of a kindly sister woman to an unhappy brother man. That was all. And he was grateful to her. Indeed, as he rode homeward, taking a winding détour that should bring him to his own gate from a direction opposite the cemetery, as the hour was late, he was conscious of a lightened burden.

The tension of awful secrecy had been eased by the simple sharing of it with another—another who, notwithstanding her own different temperament, "understood."

This was Elijah's mood to-day; but when next morning came he found himself definitely annoyed at the thought of the interested woman in the cemetery. She would know when he came in and went out. Maybe she would be watching while he buried the bud. He would feel like such a fool if he suspected this. He hoped that, having once been kind and neighborly, she would henceforth mind her own business and let him alone.

Fortunately for his state of mind, there was no reason to fear that she was anywhere near on this first day, and he performed his mission without any sort of disturbance—excepting, indeed, the distinct irritation he felt when he perceived the bent hair-pin still lying where she had dropped it the day before.

The color mounted to his face when he saw this, and if the widow had appeared before him at this moment it would have been hard for him.

She did not come, however. Indeed, though he regularly came and went—and always looked for her—he did not see her for several weeks; and when at last, nearly a month later, he did meet her coming in with a watering-pot in her hand, she only smiled in a simple and friendly way, as she said to him, quite as if he might have been any other man: "Good-mornin', Mr. Tomkins. Mighty dry spell o' weather," and passed on.

This was well done; and Elijah was pleased, though he was destined to experience a somewhat uncomfortable moment, as he instantly realized that he had met and spoken to a lady bearing a heavy vessel of water and had not offered to carry it for her.

Indeed, he was suddenly so ashamed of himself that he turned to proffer the tardy courtesy; but she had gone so far—and his voice did not come at the critical moment—and—well, the opportunity passed.

When it was over, he felt rather glad that his courteous impulse had failed to carry. Better let her think him a trifle remiss, or even impolite, than for him to "begin 'totin'' water to John Christian's grave."

"Ef I was to be ketched doin' sech a thing ez that," he even reflected further, "I'd be worse off 'n ever."

The summer was a long and lonely one to Elijah. His home, left to the care of a single old servant, was wellnigh comfortless.

Adam's first necessity, preserved through the very conditions of its transmission, has become the one unimpaired heritage of his latest son. It is still, even as at first, not good for man to be alone. A primary need of his life is yet the sustaining companionship of some good woman, be she wife or mother or sister or friend. And it is well for him if she be better than he; happy for him if she spice the sweetness of her relation with differences of thought and opinion. Only let him feel that she *understands* him, *and cares.*

Elijah, in spite of all her expressions of kindness to him, and her since becoming reticence, had never quite forgiven the widow Christian for discovering his secret. The rusting hairpin, always definitely located in his consciousness, even when the summer's full growth had covered it over, was still an irritation to him.

And yet, when the season of shortening days

was at hand, when September was waning and October's promise was so very barren, he one day idly wondered if he should never meet, if for but a moment's recognition—"jest for a passin' o' the time o' day"—the one woman on earth who knew *and respected* his secret; the one who, so far as her slight knowledge went, *understood* him.

He saw her again, very soon after this, but there was no greeting. He had taken a fancy to come in by "her gate," and he found she had just preceded him. For the length of such a distance as one would designate as "a block" in New York—it would be "a square" in New Orleans—he walked a short distance behind her. And the morning sun shone full upon her all the way, defining her trig figure, penetrating the coil of her hair. She did not look around, though she must have heard his step.

The widow Christian was, as already seen, a Presbyterian, and as she walked before Elijah down the gravelled path, every hair of her head seemed a fitting expression of her faith. Each strand lay as if obeying a divine injunction dating from the foundations of the world. But it was clean and wholesome, and of a true blue-black.

It was frankly Calvinistic, eminently sure, by

every declaration of its polished braid, of its calling and election.

And yet—its conscientious wearer was canonizing a drunkard, reincarnating the tares of his wasted life as flowers, and feasting her famished soul upon their fragrance and beauty, willingly self-deceived—apologizing, as the good always do to the bad. Base indeed must be a life too poor to yield a posthumous flowering of balm for the anointing of loving hearts. The inconsistency of the lonely little Presbyterian woman's daily devotions at a shrine so meagre and yet so rich in color and symbols was full of pathos. She reminded one of a little Romanist at her *prie-dieu* burning her candle for a departed soul—without the consolations of purgatory.

Elijah did not try to overtake her this morning, nor, be it quickly said to his credit, did he think these thoughts about her. They are the writer's —and idle enough.

But Elijah was touched with sympathy for her as she walked alone before him—he knew not why.

There was a suspicion of chill in the air as he sniffed its breath this morning. The faint, indescribable atmospheric relief that comes when a Southern September yawns for a minute is hard to describe. It is only as if summer were tired, perhaps. Still, a yawn always presages a new era—a renascence beyond its culmination.

To Elijah it meant that the season of the blooming rose was on the wane. He lingered quite a while at his poor shrine to-day, waiting, for no reason at all. But when he was presently startled by a rustling skirt, and, looking up, saw the widow depart, he turned away with a definite sense of disappointment.

She certainly had known he was there, and might have had the grace to look over and nod, or to remark that it was a cool morning, or a warm one. Either would have been true enough.

"The fact is," he reflected, as a fretful ten-year-old boy might have done—"the fact is, she don't keer no mo' for me 'n what she does for the next one. She was jest kind to me because she *is* kind, that's all—an' I was jest big enough of a fool to think she felt reel neighborly."

If there was reason for such misgiving to-day, the morrow brought the lonely man a goodly grain of reassurance. It was indeed a full day.

Unconsciously piqued by his last experience, he determined that it should not be repeated, and so he had risen betimes and gone earlier than usual to the cemetery; and he was turning away, feeling remote enough from all human sympathy, when he saw his neighbor enter the gate, and by first intention start in his direction. His first feeling was a qualm of apprehension lest she had set out on a visit of investigation, and would turn back when she should see him.

But no; she had seen him. There was pleased recognition of his presence in her face as she approached him. This was, by-the-way, the first time that he saw that she was pretty—or thought of it, indeed.

"I thought I'd find you here early this mornin', Mr. Tomkins, an' so I hurried up to ketch you." Such was her frank and friendly greeting. "Mr. Tomkins," she repeated, when she had reached him, "I jest wanted to tell you thet Jim Peters is goin' to be fetched down from Sandy Crik an' buried here to-morrer. The Peters lot is right down there back o' yours, an' the men are comin' by sunup in the mornin' to dig his grave; an' I thought maybe, like ez not, you'd like to know it. I know you'd likely ruther not meet 'em here. Ef you don't feel like gittin' up about three o'clock—it's high moon then—why, you could easy slip around after sundown. They don't never be anybody here late of evenin's nohow. I often come in an' sprinkle his pansies after the sun's off of 'em, an' I never have met nobody here 'long about dark."

She stood facing the grave on the side opposite

Elijah as she spoke. There was a note of simple friendliness in her voice, and it touched him deeply.

"I declare, Mis' Christian," he said, with emotion, "I do think you're the best-hearted an' kindest lady I've ever knew in all my life. I do indeed." And then, as his eyes fell upon the grave between them, he hastened to add, "Present company excepted, of co'se."

"Of co'se," she repeated in generous assent. "An' I respect you all the mo' for that polite attention to her, Mr. Tomkins. They ain't many men that would 'a' done it." And then she added: "I see thet you 'ain't never come over to his square sence that one time. You ought to walk in some time when I ain't there to bother you, even ef you don't need to borry the hedge, jest to see how purty it is. Them pansies have turned out lovely. But the funniest thing happened. Right in the row with the black-faced ones—jest about where you set that mornin'—would you believe it thet one o' them pansies bloomed out pink? Ever' one planted from dead-black seeds, mind you. An' do you know, maybe I ought to 've picked it out quick ez it showed color, but I didn't. I *couldn't do it*, Mr. Tomkins. Seemed to me that pansy stood out there jest to remind me o' the day thet I was

"'PRESENT COMPANY EXCEPTED'"

enabled to cheer you up a little, an' whenever I'd look into its sassy little pink face with its quizzical eyebrows I'd seem to see you a-settin' there shakin' with laughter. An' it's done me good, too. When the good Lord sends a little thing like that out o' His ground, where He works so much magic for the comfort of our hearts, I believe in jest takin' it ez He sends it. An' that pansy plant has kep' a pink face there for me all summer ; an' when I'd look at it I'd often remember to wish a little wish for you, Mr. Tomkins. I've often wanted to ask how yore two babies was comin' on, but I didn't like to. But ef I'd knew you well enough when she died, I wouldn't no mo' have advised you to let yore sister take them children out o' yore house than nothin'. Ef they's ever a time a man needs his child'en it is when their mother is took away. Goin' to see 'em once-t a week the way you do ain't *livin'*. If *I* was *you*, an' them *my* babies, well— Howsoever, excuse me for meddlin'. Maybe ef I'd ever had any child'en o' my own they wouldn't seem like gold an' diamonds to me the way they do. But here I keep on a-talkin'. It's a little fresh this mornin', an' I reckon we'll have the early frost. Sech buds ez you find now must be most too pretty to bury. Fall roses always seem like they put on their purtiest so ez to make you hate to see 'em go. *Good*-bye."

Instead of answering, Elijah stepped quickly around the grave and joined her.

"Don't hurry away, Mis' Christian," he said, as he stepped beside her. "I 'ain't got no nice seat to offer you, like you have, but I want to talk to you a little. It's been on my mind some time to tell you thet you mustn't think I 'ain't got no mo' pride than to let this grave o' mine all run to weeds forever. I'm jest a-waitin' a little—tell it settles solid—an' I'm goin' to have it fixed up decent an' expensive. I thought about havin' a reg'lar long slab laid down over it, an' all cemented round the edges. But I won't do it now tell all the buds give out. I've got so used to layin' the bud under the sod thet I wouldn't feel ez ef she had it ef it was on top a lot o' marble an' stuff. She was a mighty good wife, Mis' Christian—most of her time porely, ez you know. They's many a little thing I wisht I'd 'a' done for her, ez I look back. I'd 'a' had a marble stone there long ago—'ceptin' for the buds."

"Well—I don't know but you're wise, Mr. Tomkins. Sometimes I thought of cementin' *his* in, an' jest lettin' it rest so. But I haven't never been able to make up my mind what I'd do with the bottles—whether I'd leave 'em inside or take 'em out. Sometimes," she sighed, and hesitated—"*some* times I have reel strange misgivin's about them bottles. Supposin', f' instance, thet at the resurrection he was to be shamed out of all countenance findin' 'em here—with the brewer's name blowed in each one—an' all the white ribboned angels a-flyin' round. Of co'se *we* can't tell how things is goin' to be—an' they're *bound* to be *some* way. I don't know but I'll change it all yet—some day. But ef I *was* to cement him in I'd feel mighty empty-handed—an' lost. But reely, Mr. Tomkins, instid o' you apologizin' to *me*, I want to tell you thet I've often felt reproached seein' you slip in an' out so reg'lar an' so quiet. You're doin' a thing she *ast* you to do—an' doin' it modest and sincere. An' me — I'm doin' a thing he never would 'a' liked in creation, an' makin' a show of it—though how it would look was cert'nly the last thing on earth in my mind. Somehow pore John never stood ez high ez I'd liked him to among the livin' an' I have been ambitious to have him stand well among the dead. But you're the only human I've ever spoke to about it, an' the good Lord knows you're the last man I'd 'a' ever thought I could 'a' spoke to—seven months ago. We never know what we'll do—tell it's done."

They were at the opening of the hedge now, and she walked in, Tomkins following.

"Ef you want to see yoreself ez others see you, or at least ez I saw you, Mr. Tomkins, look at this pink pansy."

She chuckled merrily as she turned the saucy face of the flower so that he could see it. Tomkins laughed too as he looked at it.

"Nobody knows how much company them pink faces have been to me all summer. Croppin' out there in the black row they're like jokes at a funeral. We've all told 'em — or listened to 'em—an' they's no place on earth thet a joke gets its own more'n at a funeral, to my thinkin'. Yas, ez I said, Mr. Tomkins— Set down a minute, won't you? I won't charge you any more."

Her playful mood was like wine to poor Elijah after a long thirst. She moved to the end of the bench to make room for him, and he sat down.

"Yas, ez I said," she began, in quite a changed tone, and yet with a spring in her voice—"ez I said, Mr. Tomkins, I'd have them babies home—*ef they was mine*—sister or no sister. Why, the way you're a-living now, you ain't no mo'n a uncle to 'em. An' the way *I* look at it—of co'se you ain't never goin' to think of marryin' again; you are like me in that—an' so, the way you start out with them child'n o' yores is likely to continue. Ef you was jest holdin' off tell sech a time ez you could turn out among the girls to pick out a step-mother for 'em for her rosy cheeks, it would be different. Yore sister would do jest ez well ez anybody else to ripen 'em for her. But it seems to me thet a man o' yore standin' an' yore stren'th o' mind would 'a' took some nice pious old lady like Mis' Gibbs, f' instance, thet has done quilted all her life away nearly, an' won't accept no home thet she can't earn. Seems to me sech a lady ez that would 'a' kep' yo' family circle intac'—an' earned a good home at the same time. An' Mis' Gibbs, why, she thinks the world an' all of you. She grannied yore mother when you was born—maybe you remember—'t least so she says. She says you was the reddest baby she ever see in her life, but I sort o' doubt that—with yore brown hair."

She glanced at Elijah's head as she spoke.

"Well!" she laughed; "don't know ez I doubt it, either, look at you now."

He had, indeed, blushed scarlet, and now he blushed again because she had noticed it.

"I do declare!" she laughed again. "I reckon you must be like a girl I went to school with. She always said she felt humiliated every time she reelized she'd ever been a baby. But I glory in it. The only grudge I've got against it is thet I can't *remember* how folks fed me an' dressed me an' toted me around—waited on me. I 'ain't got a single ricollection of sech ez thet in all my life—not a one. I've done the fetchin' and carryin' for others ever sence I can remember, an' done it willin' enough, too. Still, I'm glad to know thet I have had my innin's. But you think over what I've said about ole Mis' Gibbs now—but don't never let on thet I mentioned it. Some child'en is afeerd of her on account of her wig—but they'd soon git used to it. It does shift some sence she's fell away so, but I don't doubt thet at the head o' yore bountiful table she'd very soon grow up to it again. I know what one broke-up home is, Mr. Tomkins, an' I hate to see another. Mine can't help but stay broke—'less'n I'd start adoptin', which would be a hard thing to do—in Simpkinsville. There couldn't never possibly be a orphan without relations here, where everybody is kin—an' a orphan with about twenty-'leven lookers-on is the last thing on earth for anybody to adopt."

This was the last meeting Elijah had with the widow Christian during this season. He stayed a few minutes to-day, her willing listener and grateful guest.

When he finally made his awkward adieus his

mind was filled with a new hope in her suggestion of reconstructing his broken circle—bringing his children home. Perhaps, after all, *all* of life had not gone out of living.

He wished a little, as he pondered over her plan, that old Mrs. Gibbs's wig were a closer fit, and that she were, perhaps, a trifle less reminiscent. But these were externalities. She would really care for him—and his babes. There would be a light in the front room when he should go home at night.

As he looked back over the last seven months, Elijah felt as if he had always been a widower—and wretched. It must be wretched to be a widower, else why the common race for escape?

Perhaps widowhood is as miserable, but its pangs are different, being matters of a woman's soul. With her it is rarely a question of home-breaking or bodily discomfort. She is herself a maker and disburser of comfort. Where she is is home. And so her sorrow is—otherwise.

The more Elijah pondered over the question of reorganizing his home, the more the desire to do so grew strong within him.

Still—so irreconcilable are sometimes the factors in a difficult situation—the more he thought of old Mrs. Gibbs seated with wig askew behind his coffee-urn, the less the picture invited his consent.

But the new concept had taken shape—a reorganized family table—a little chair on one side—a high chair on the other. If old Mrs. Gibbs's wig bobbed up constantly behind the coffee-urn, there was at least an interrogation point above it. And in the interrogation there is hope.

Elijah was very thoughtful these days—very circumspect—very serious.

Many times he went to the cemetery, paid his tribute, and came away without even looking towards the Christian lot.

Perhaps he was thinking of old Mrs. Gibbs.

However this may be, a few days after this last interview, when he had, as usual, deposited his floral tribute, he leaned over the grave, and reaching forward, felt carefully about the roots of a certain clump of grass, as if searching for something, and presently he picked up an old, very rusty hair-pin.

He laid it in the palm of his other hand a moment and looked at it. Then, taking his handkerchief, he wiped it tenderly, as if it were a precious thing.

"I don't know what on earth I been a-thinkin'

about to let it all go to rust that-a-way," he said, aloud.

And then he carefully put it in his pocket.*

* The writer wishes to say that this is positively all that ever happened between the widow Christian and Elijah Tomkins, bereaved, in the Simpkinsville cemetery, and the report that went abroad at the time of their marriage, some months later, to the effect that they had begun their courting in the graveyard, is utterly without foundation in fact. And she trusts the impartial reader to agree that never were two mateless mourners more circumspect, never two with time and abundant opportunity who were more loyal to their respective dead, than they.

THE UNLIVED LIFE OF LITTLE MARY ELLEN

THE UNLIVED LIFE OF LITTLE MARY ELLEN

WHEN Simpkinsville sits in shirt-sleeves along her store fronts in summer, she does not wish to be considered *en déshabillé.* Indeed, excepting in extreme cases, she would—after requiring that you translate it into plain American, perhaps—deny the soft impeachment.

Simpkinsville knows about coats, and she knows about ladies, and she knows that coats and ladies are to be taken together.

But there are hot hours during August when nothing should be required to be taken with anything—unless, indeed, it be ice—with everything excepting more ice.

During the long afternoons in fly-time no woman who has any discretion—or, as the Simpkinsville men would say, any "management"—would leave her comfortable home to go "hangin' roun' sto'e counters to be waited on." And if they will—as they sometimes do—why, let them take the consequences.

Still, there are those who, from the simple prestige which youth and beauty give, are regarded in the Simpkinsville popular mind-masculine as belonging to a royal family before whom all things must give way—even shirt-sleeves.

For these, and because any one of them may turn her horse's head into the main road and drive up to any of the stores any hot afternoon, there are coat-pegs within easy reach upon the inside door-frames—pegs usually covered with the linen dusters and seersucker cutaways of the younger men without.

Very few of the older ones disturb themselves about these trivial matters. Even the doctors, of whom there are two in town, both "leading physicians," are wont to receive their most important "office patients" in this comfortable fashion as, palmetto fans in hand, they rise from their comfortable chairs, tilted back against the weather-boarded fronts of their respective drug-stores, and step forward to the buggies of such ladies as drive up for quinine and capsules, or to present their ailing babies for open-air glances at their throats or gums, without so much as displacing their linen lap-robes.

When any of the village belles drive or walk past, such of the commercial drummers as may be sitting trigly coated, as they sometimes do, among the shirt-sleeves, have a way of feeling of their ties and bringing the front legs of their chairs to the floor, while they sit forward in supposed parlor attitudes, and easily doff their hats with a grace that the Simpkinsville boys fiercely denounce while they vainly strive to imitate it.

A country boy's hat will not take on that repose which marks the cast of the metropolitan hatter, let him try to command it as he may.

It was peculiarly hot and sultry to-day in Simpkinsville, and business was abnormally dull —even the apothecary business—this being the annual mid-season's lull between spring fevers and green chinquapins.

Old Dr. Alexander, after nodding for an hour over his fan beneath his tarnished gilt sign of the pestle and mortar, had strolled diagonally across the street to join his friend and *confrère*, Dr. Jenkins, in a friendly chat.

The doctors were not much given to this sort of sociability, but sometimes when times were unbearably dull and healthy, and neither was called to any one else, they would visit one another and talk to keep awake.

"Well, I should say so!" The visitor dropped

into the vacant chair beside his host as he spoke. "I should say so. Ain't it hot enough *for you?* Ef it ain't, I'd advise you to renounce yo' religion an' prepare for a climate thet 'll suit you."

This pleasantry was in reply to the common summer-day greeting. "Hot enough for you to-day, doc'?"

"Yas," continued the guest, as he zigzagged the back legs of his chair forward by quick jerks until he had gained the desired leaning angle—"Yas, it's too hot to live, an' not hot enough to die. I reckon that's why we have so many chronics a-hangin' on."

"Well, don't let's quarrel with sech as the Lord provides, doctor," replied his host, with a chuckle. "Ef it wasn't for the chronics, I reckon you an' I'd have to give up practisin' an' go to makin' soap. Ain't that about the size of it?"

"Yas, chronics an'—an' babies. Ef *they* didn't come so punctual, summer an' winter, I wouldn't be able to feed mine thet 're a'ready here. But talkin' about the chronics, do you know, doctor, thet sometimes when I don't have much else to think about, why, I think about them. It's a strange providence to me thet keeps people a-hangin' on year in an' year out, neither sick nor well. I don't doubt the Almighty's goodness, of co'se; but we've got Scripture for callin'

Him the Great Physician, an' why, when He could ef He would, He don't—"

"I wouldn't dare to ask myself sech questions as that, doctor, ef I was you. *I* wouldn't, I know. Besides"—and now he laughed—"besides, I jest give you a reason for lettin' 'em remain as they are—to feed us poor devils of doctors. An' besides that, I've often seen cases where it seemed to me they were allowed to live to sanctify them thet had to live *with* 'em. Of co'se in this I'm not speakin' of great sufferers. An' no doubt they all get pretty tired an' wo'e out with themselves sometimes. I do with myself, even, an' I'm well. Jest listen at them boys a-whistlin' 'After the Ball' to Brother Binney's horse's trot! They haven't got no mo' reverence for a minister o' the gospel than nothin'. I s'pose as long as they ricollect his preachin' against dancin' they'll make him ride into town to that sort o' music. They've made it up among 'em to do it. Jest listen—all the way up the street that same tune. An' Brother Binney trottin' in smilin' to it."

While they were talking the Rev. Mr. Binney rode past, and following, a short distance behind him, came a shabby buggy, in which a shabby woman sat alone. She held her reins a trifle high as she drove, and it was this somewhat awkward position which revealed the fact, even as she approached in the distance, that she carried what seemed an infant lying upon her lap.

"There comes the saddest sight in Simpkinsville, doctor. I notice them boys stop their whistlin' jest as soon as her buggy turned into the road. I'm glad there's some things they respect," said Dr. Alexander.

"Yas, and I see the fellers at Rowton's sto'e are goin' in for their coats. She's drawin' rein there now."

"Yas, but she ain't more'n leavin' an order, I reckon. She's comin' this way."

The shabby buggy was bearing down upon them now, indeed, and when Dr. Jenkins saw it he too rose and put on his coat. As its occupant drew rein he stepped out to her side, while his companion, having raised his hat, looked the other way.

"Get out an' come in, Mis' Bradley." Dr. Jenkins had taken her hand as he spoke.

"No, thanky, doctor. 'Taint worth while. I jest want to consult you about little Mary Ellen. She ain't doin' well, some ways."

At this she drew back the green barége veil that was spread over the bundle upon her lap, exposing, as she did so, the blond head and

"'GET OUT AN' COME IN, MIS' BRADLEY'"

chubby face of a great wax doll, with eyes closed as if in sleep.

The doctor laid the veil back in its place quickly.

"I wouldn't expose her face to the evenin' sun, Mis' Bradley," he said, gently. "I'll call out an' see her to-morrow; an' ef I was you I think I'd keep her indoors for a day or so." Then as he glanced into the woman's haggard and eager face, he added: "She's gettin' along as well as might be expected, Mis' Bradley. But I'll be out to-morrow, an' fetch you somethin' thet 'll put a little color in *yo'* face."

"Oh, don't mind me, doctor," she answered, with a sigh of relief, as she tucked the veil carefully under the little head. "Don't mind me. I ain't sick. Ef I could jest see *her* pick up a little, why, I'd feel all right. When you come to-morrer, better fetch somethin' *she* can take, doctor. Well, good-bye."

"Good-bye, Mis' Bradley."

It was some moments before either of the doctors spoke after Dr. Jenkins had returned to his place. And then it was he who said:

"Talkin' about the ways o' Providence, doctor, what do you call that?"

"That's one o' the mysteries thet it's hard to unravel, doctor. Ef anything would make me doubt the mercy of God Almighty, it would be some sech thing as that. And yet—I don't know. Ef there ever was a sermon preached without words, there's one preached along the open streets of Simpkinsville by that pore little half-demented woman when she drives into town nursin' that wax doll. An' it's preached where it's much needed, too—to our young people. There ain't many preachers that can reach 'em, but— Did you take notice jest now how, as soon as she turned into the road, all that whistlin' stopped? They even neglected to worry Brother Binney. An' she's the only woman in town thet 'll make old Rowton put on a coat. He'll wait on yo' wife or mine in his shirt-sleeves, an' it's all right. But there's somethin' in that broken-hearted woman nursin' a wax doll thet even a fellow like Rowton 'll feel. Didn't you ever think thet maybe you ought to write her case up, doctor?"

"Yas; an' I've done it—as far as it goes. I've called it 'A Psychological Impossibility.' An' then I've jest told her story. A heap of impossible things have turned out to be facts—facts that had to be argued backward from. You can do over argiments, but you can't undo facts. Yas, I've got her case all stated as straight as I can state it, an' some day it 'll be read. But not while she's livin'. Sir? No, not even with names changed an' everything. It wouldn't do. It couldn't help bein' traced back to her. No; some day, when we've all passed away, likely, it 'll all come out in a medical journal, signed by me. An' I've been thinkin' thet I'd like to have you go over that paper with me some time, doctor, so thet you could testify to it. An' I thought we'd get Brother Binney to put his name down as the minister thet had been engaged to perform the marriage, an' knew all the ins and outs of it. And then it 'll hardly be believed."

Even as they spoke they heard the whistling start up again along the street, and, looking up, they saw the Rev. Mr. Binney approaching.

"We've jest been talkin' about you, Brother Binney—even before the boys started you to dancin'." Dr. Jenkins rose and brought out a third chair.

"No," answered the dominie, as with a good-natured smile he dismounted. "No, they can't make me dance, an' I don't know as it's a thing my mare 'll have to answer for. She seems to take naturally to the sinful step, an' so, quick as they start a-whistlin', I try to ride as upright an' godly as I can, to sort o' equalize things. How were you two discussin' me, I'd like to know?"

He put the question playfully as he took his seat.

"Well, we were havin' a pretty serious talk, brother," said Dr. Jenkins—"a pretty serious talk, doc and me. We were talkin' about pore Miss Mary Ellen. We were sayin' thet we reckoned ef there were any three men in town thet were specially qualified to testify about her case, we must be the three—you an' him an' me. I've got it all written out, an' I thought some day I'd get you both to read it over an' put your names to it, with any additions you might feel disposed to make. After we've all passed away, there ought to be some authorized account. You know about as much as we do, I reckon, Brother Binney."

"Yes, I s'pose I do—in a way. I stood an' watched her face durin' that hour an' a quarter they stood in church waitin' for Clarence Bradley to come. Mary Ellen never was to say what you'd call a purty girl, but she always did have a face thet would hold you ef you ever looked at it. An' when she stood in church that day, with all her bridesmaids strung around the chancel, her countenance would 'a' done for any heavenly picture. An' as the time passed, an' he didn't show up— Well, I don't want to compare sinfully, but there's a picture I saw once of Mary at the

Cross— Reckon I ought to take that back, lest it might be sinful; but there ain't any wrong in my telling you here thet as I stood out o' sight, waitin' that day in church, behind the pyramid o' flowers the bridesmaids had banked up for her, with my book open in my hand at the marriage service, while we waited for him to come, as she stood before the pulpit in her little white frock and wreath, I could see her face. An' there came a time, after it commenced to get late, when I fell on my knees."

The good man stopped speaking for a minute to steady his voice.

"You see," he resumed, presently, "we'd all heard things. I *knew* he'd *seemed* completely taken up with this strange girl; an' when at last he came for me to marry him and Mary Ellen, I never was so rejoiced in my life. Thinks I, I've been over-suspicious. Of co'se I knew he an' Mary Ellen had been sweethearts all their lives. I tell you, friends, I've officiated at funerals in my life—buried little children an' mothers of families—an' I've had my heart in my throat so thet I could hardly do my duty; but I tell you I never in all my life had as sad an experience as I did at little Mary Ellen Williams's weddin'—the terrible, terrible weddin' thet never came off."

"An' I've had patients," said Dr. Jenkins, coming into the pause—"I've had patients, Brother Binney, thet I've lost—lost 'em because the time had come for 'em to die—patients thet I've grieved to see go more as if I was a woman than a man, let alone a doctor; but I never in all my life come so near *clair* givin' way an' breakin' down as I did at that weddin' when you stepped out an' called me out o' the congregation to tell me she had fainted. God help us, it was terrible! I'll never forget that little white face as it lay so limpy and still against the lilies tied to the chancel rail, not ef I live a thousand years. Of co'se we'd all had our fears, same as you. We knew Clarence's failin', an' we saw how the yaller-haired girl had turned his head; but, of co'se, when it come to goin' into the church, why, we thought it was all right. But even after the thing had happened—even knowin' as much as I did—I never to say fully took in the situation till the time come for her to get better. For two weeks she lay 'twixt life an' death, an' the one hope I had was for her to recognize me. She hadn't recognized anybody since she was brought out o' the church. But when at last she looked at me one day, an' says she, 'Doctor—what you reckon kep' him—so late?' I tell you I can't tell you how I felt."

"What did you say, doctor?"

It was the minister who ventured the question.

"What can a man say when he 'ain't got nothin' to say? I jest said, 'Better not talk any to-day, honey.' An' I turned away an' made pertence o' mixin' powders—*an'* mixed 'em, for that matter—give her sech as would put her into a little sleep. An' then I set by her till she drowsed away. But when she come out o' that sleep an' I see how things was—when she called herself Mis' Bradley an' kep' askin' for him, an' I see she didn't know no better, an' likely never would—God help me! but even while I prescribed physic for her to live, in my heart I prayed to see her die. She thought she had been married, an' from that day to this she 'ain't never doubted it. Of co'se she often wonders why he don't come home; an' sence that doll come, she—"

"Didn't it ever strike you as a strange providence about that doll—thet would allow sech a thing, for instance, doctor?"

Dr. Jenkins did not answer at once.

"Well," he said, presently, "yas—yas an' no. Ef a person looks at it *close-t enough*, it 'ain't so hard to see mercy in God's judgments. I happened to be at her bedside the day that doll come in—Christmas Eve four years ago. She was mighty weak an' porely. She gen'ally gets down in bed 'long about the holidays, sort o' reelizin' the passin' o' time, seein' he don't come. She had been so werried and puny thet the old nigger 'Pollo come for me to see her. An', well, while I set there tryin' to think up somethin' to help her, 'Pollo, he fetched in the express package."

"I've always blamed her brother, Brother Binney," Dr. Alexander interposed, "for *allowin'* that package to go to her."

"*Allowin'!* Why, he never allowed it. You might jest as well say you blame him for namin' his one little daughter after her aunt Mary Ellen. That's how the mistake was made. No, for my part I never thought so much of Ned Williams in my life as I did when he said to me the day that baby girl was born, 'Ef it's a girl, doctor, we're a-goin' to name it after sis' Mary Ellen. Maybe it 'll be a comfort to her.' An' they did. How many brothers, do you reckon, would name a child after a sister thet had lost her mind over a man thet had jilted her at the church door, an' called herself by his name ever sence? Not many, I reckon. No, don't blame Ned—for anything. He hoped she'd love the little thing, an' maybe it would help her. An' she did notice it consider'ble for a while, but it didn't seem to have the power to bring her mind straight. In fact, the way she'd set an' look at it for hours, an' then go home an' set down an' seem to be thinkin', makes me sometimes suspicion thet that was what started her a-prayin' God to send her a child. She's said to me more than once-t about that time—she'd say, 'You see, doctor, when he's away so much—ef it was God's will—a child would be a heap o' company to me while he's away.' This, mind you, when he hadn't shown up at the weddin'; when we all knew he ran away an' married the yaller-hair that same night. Of co'se it did seem a strange providence to be sent to a God-fearin' woman as she always was; it did seem strange thet she should be allowed to make herself redic'lous carryin' that wax doll around the streets; an' yet, when you come to think—"

"Well, I say what I did befo'," said Dr. Alexander. "Her brother should 'a' *seen* to it thet no sech express package intended for his child should 'a' been sent to the aunt—not in her state o' mind."

"How could he see to it when he didn't send it—didn't know it was comin'? Of co'se we Simpkinsville folks, we all know thet she's called Mary Ellen, an' thet Ned's child has been nicknamed Nellie. But his wife's kin, livin' on the other side o' the continent, they couldn't be expected to know that, an' when they sent her that doll, why, they nachelly addressed it to her full name; an' it was sent up to Miss Mary Ellen's. Even then the harm needn't to 've been done exceptin' for her bein' sick abed, an' me, her doctor, hopin' to enliven her up a little with an unexpected present, makes the nigger 'Pollo set it down by her bedside, and opens it befo' her eyes, right there. Maybe I'm to blame for that—*but I ain't*. We can't do mo' than *try* for the best. I thought likely as not Ned had ordered her some little Christmas things—as he had, in another box."

The old doctor stopped, and, taking out his handkerchief, wiped his eyes.

"Of co'se, as soon as I see what it was, I knew somebody had sent it to little Mary Ellen, but—

"You say, Brother Binney, thet the look in her face at the weddin' made you fall on yo' knees. I wish you could 'a' seen the look thet come into her eyes when I lifted that doll-baby out of that box. Heavenly Father! That look is one o' the things thet 'll come back to me sometimes when I wake up too early in the mornin's, an' I can't get back to sleep for it. But at the time I didn't fully realize it, somehow. She jest reached an' took the doll out o' my hands, an' turnin' over, with her face to the wall, held it tight in her arms without sayin' a word. Then she lay still for so long that-a-way thet by-an'-bye I commenced to get uneasy less'n she'd fainted. So I leaned over an' felt of her pulse, an' I see she was layin' there cryin' over it without a sound—an' I come away. I don't know how came I to be so thick-headed, but even then I jest supposed thet seein' the doll nachelly took her mind back to the time she was a child, an' that in itself was mighty sad an' pitiful to me, knowin' her story, and I confess to you I was glad there wasn't anybody I had to speak to on my way out. I tell you I was about cryin' myself—jest over the pitifulness of even that. But next day when I went back of co'se I see how it was. She never had doubted for a minute thet that doll was the baby she'd been prayin' for—not a minute. An' she don't, *not to this day*—straight as her mind is on some things. That's why I call it a psychological impossibility, she bein' so rational an' so crazy at the same time. Sent for me only last week, an' when I got there I found her settin' down with *it* a-layin' in her lap, an' she lookin' the very picture of despair. 'Doctor,' says she, 'I'm sure they's mo' wrong with Mary Ellen than you let on to me. *She don't grow, doctor.*' An' with that she started a-sobbin' an' a-rockin' back an' fo'th over it. 'An' even the few words she could say, doctor, she seems to forget 'em,' says she. 'She 'ain't called my name for a week.' It's a fact; the little talkin'-machine inside it has got out o' fix some way, an' it don't say 'mamma' and 'papa' any mo'."

"Have you ever thought about slippin' it away from her, doctor, an' seein' if maybe she wouldn't forget it? If she was my patient I'd try it."

"Yas, but you wouldn't keep it up. I did try it once-t. Told old Milly thet ef she fretted too much not to give her the doll, but to send for me. An' she did—in about six hours. An' I—well, when I see her face I jest give it back to her. An' I'll never be the one to take it from her again. It comes nearer givin' her happiness than anything else could—an' what could be mo' innocent? She's even mo' contented since her mother died an' there ain't anybody to prevent her carryin' it on the street. I know it plegged Ned at first to see her do it, but he's never said a word. He's one in a thousand. He cares mo' for his sister's happiness than for how she looks to other folks. Most brothers don't. There ain't a mornin' but he drives in there to see ef she wants anything, an', of co'se, keepin' up the old place jest for her to live in it costs him consider'ble. He says she wouldn't allow it, but she thinks Clarence pays for everything, an' of co'se he was fully able."

"I don't think it's a good way for her to live, doctor, in that big old place with jest them two old niggers. I never have thought so. Ef she was *my* patient—"

"Well, pardner, that's been talked over between Ned an' his wife, an' they've even consulted me. An' I b'lieve she ought to be let alone. Those two old servants take about as good care of her as anybody could. Milly nursed her when she was a baby, an' she loves the ground she walks on, an' she humors her in everything. Why, I've gone out there an' found that old nigger walkin' that doll up an' down the po'ch, singing to it for all she was worth; an' when I'd drive up, the po' ol' thing would cry so she couldn't go in the house for ten minutes or mo'. No, it ain't for us to take away sech toys as the Lord sends to comfort an' amuse his little ones; an' the weak-minded, why, they always seem that-a-way to me. An' sometimes, when I come from out of some of our homes where everything is regular and straight accordin' to our way o' lookin' at things, an' I see how miserable an' unhappy everything *is*, an' I go out to the old Williams place, where the birds are singin' in the trees an' po' Miss Mary Ellen is happy sewin' her little doll-clo'es, an' the old niggers ain't got a care on earth but to look after her— Well, I dun'no'. Ef you'd dare say the love o' God wasn't there, *I* wouldn't. Of co'se she has her unhappy moments, an' I can see she's failin' as time passes; but even so, ain't *this* for the best? They'd be somethin' awful about it, *to me*, ef she kep' a-growin' stronger through it all. One o' the sweetest providences o' sorrow is thet we poor mortals fail under it. There ain't a flower thet blooms but some seed has perished for it."

It was at a meeting of the woman's prayer-meeting, about a week after the conversation just related, that Mrs. Blanks, the good sister who led the meeting, rose to her feet, and, after a silence that betokened some embarrassment in the subject she essayed, said:

"My dear sisters, I've had a subjec' on my mind for a long time, a subjec' thet I've hesitated to mention, but the mo' I put it away the mo' it seems to come back to me. I've hesitated because she's got kinfolks in this prayer-meetin', but I don't believe thet there's anybody kin to Miss Mary Ellen thet feels any nearer to her than what the rest of us do."

"Amen!" "Amen!" and "Amen!" came in

timid women's voices from different parts of the room.

"I know how you all feel befo' you answer me, my dear sisters," she continued, presently. "And now I propose to you thet we, first here as a body of worshippers, an' then separately as Christian women at home in our closets, make her case a subjec' of special prayer. Let us ask the good Lord to relieve her—jest so—*unconditionally;* to take this cloud off her life an' this sorrow off our streets, an' I believe He'll do it."

There were many quiet tears shed in the little prayer-meeting that morning as, with faltering voice, one woman after another spoke her word of exhortation or petition in behalf of the long-suffering sister.

That this revival of the theme by the wives and mothers of the community should have resulted in renewed attentions to the poor distraught woman was but natural. It is sound orthodoxy to try to help God to answer our prayers. And so the faithful women of the churches—there were a few of every denomination in town in the union prayer-meeting—began to go to her, fully resolved to say some definite word to win her, if possible, from her hallucination, to break the spell that held her; but they would almost invariably come away full of contrition over such false and comforting words as they had been constrained to speak "over a soulless and senseless doll."

Indeed, a certain Mrs. Lynde, one of the most ardent of these good women, but a sensitive soul withal, was moved, after one of her visits, to confess in open meeting both her sin and her chagrin in the following humiliating fashion:

"I declare I never felt so 'umbled in my life ez I did after I come away from there, a week ago come Sunday. Here I goes, full of clear reasonin' an' Scripture texts, to try to bring her to herself, an' I 'ain't no mo'n set down sca'cely, when I looks into her face, as she sets there an' po's out her sorrers over that ridic'lous little doll, befo' I'm consolin' her with false hopes, like a perfec' Ananias an' Sapphira. Ef any woman could set down an' see her look at that old doll's face when she says, 'Honey, do you reckon I'll ever raise her, when she keeps so puny?'—I say ef any woman with a human heart in her bosom could hear her say that, an' not tell her, 'Cert'n'y she'd raise her,' an' that 'punier children than that had growed up to be healthy men an' women'—well, maybe they might be better Christians than I am, but I don't never expec' to be sanctified up to that point. I know I'm an awful sinner, deservin' of eternal punishment for deceit which is the same as a lie, but I not only told her I thought she could raise her, but I felt her pulse, an' said it wasn't quite what a reel hearty child's ought to be. Of co'se I said that jest to save myself from p'int-blank lyin'. An' then, when I see how it troubled her to think it wasn't *jest right,* why, God forgive me, but I felt it over again, an' counted it by my watch, an' then I up an' told her it was *all right,* an' thet ef it had a-been any different to the way it was under the circumstances, I'd be awful fearful, which, come to think of it, that last is true ez God's word, for ef I'd a-felt a pulse in that doll's wrist—which, tell the truth, I was so excited while she watched me I half expected to feel it pulsate—I'd 'a' shot out o' that door a ravin' lunatic. I come near enough a-doin' it when she patted its chest an' it said 'mamma' an' 'papa' in reply. I don't know, but I think thet the man thet put words into a doll's breast, to be hugged out by a poor, bereft, weak-minded woman, has a terrible sin to answer for. Seems to me it's a-breakin' the second commandment, which forbids the makin' of anything in the likeness of anything in the heavens above or the earth beneath, which a baby is if it's anything, bein' the breath o' God fresh-breathed into human clay. I don't know, but I think that commandment is aimed jest as direct at talkin' dolls ez it is at heathen idols, which, when you come to think of it, ain't p'intedly made after the image of anything *in* creation thet we've seen samples of, after all. Them thet I've seen the pictures of ain't no mo'n sech outlandish deformities thet anybody could conceive of ef he imagined a strange-figgured person standin' befo' a cracked merror so ez to have his various an' sundry parts duplicated, promiscuous. No, I put down the maker of that special an' partic'lar doll ez a greater idolitor than them thet, for the want o' knowin' better, stick a few extry members on a clay statute an' pray to it *in faith.* Ef it hadn't a-called her 'mamma' first time she over-squeezed it, I don't believe *for a minute* thet that doll would ever 'a' got the holt upon Mary Ellen thet it has—I don't indeed."

"Still"—it was Mrs. Blanks who spoke up in reply, wiping her eyes as she began—"still, Sister Lynde, you know she frets over it jest ez much sence it's lost its speech."

"Of co'se," said another sister; "an' why shouldn't she? Ef yo' little Katie had a-started talkin' an' then stopped of a suddent, wouldn't you 'a' been worried, I like to know?"

"Yas, I reckon I would," replied Mrs. Blanks;

"but it's hard to put her in the place of a mother with a reel child—even in a person's imagination."

There had been in Simpkinsville an occasional doll whose eyes would open and shut as she was put to bed or taken up, and the crying doll was not a thing unknown.

That the one which should play so conspicuous a part in her history should have developed the gift of speech, invested it with a weird and peculiar interest.

It was, indeed, most uncanny and sorrowful to hear its poor piping response to the distraught woman's caresses as she pressed it to her bosom.

To the little doll-loving girls of Simpkinsville it had always been an object of semi-superstitious reverence—a thing half doll, half human, almost alive.

When her little niece Nellie, a tall girl of eight years now, would come over in the mornings and beg Aunt Mary Ellen to let her hold the baby, she never quite knew, as she walked it up and down the yard, under the mulberry-trees, with the green veil laid lovingly over its closed lids, whether to look for a lapse from its human quality into ordinary dollhood, or to expect a sudden development on the life side.

She would, no doubt, long ago have lost this last hope, in the lack of progression in its mechanical speech, but for the repeated confidences of her aunt Mary Ellen.

"Why, honey, she often laughs out loud an' turns over in bed, an' sometimes she wakes me up cryin' so pitiful." So the good aunt, who had never told a lie in all her pious life, often assured her—assured her with a look in her face that was absolutely invincible in its expression of perfect faith in the thing she said.

There had been several serious conferences between her father and mother in the beginning, before the child had been allowed to go to see Aunt Mary Ellen's dolly—to see and hold it, and inevitably to love it with all her child heart; but even before the situation had developed its full sadness, or they had realized how its contingencies would familiarize every one with the strange, sad story, the arguments were in the child's favor. To begin with, the doll was really hers, though it was thought best, in the circumstances, that she should never know it. Indeed, at first her father had declared that she should have one just like it; but when it was found that its price was nearly equal to the value of a bale of cotton, the good man was moved to declare that "the outlandish thing, with its heathenish imitations, had wrought sorrer enough in the family a'ready without trying to duplicate it."

Still, there couldn't be any harm in letting her see the beautiful toy. And so, as she held it in her arms, the child came vaguely to realize that a great mystery of anxious love hovered about this strange, weird doll, a mystery that, to her young perception, as she read it in the serious home faces, was as full of tragic possibilities as that which concerned the real baby sister that lay and slept and waked and grew in the home cradle—the real, warm, heavy baby that she was sometimes allowed to hold "just for a minute" while the nurse-mammy followed close beside her.

If the toy-baby gave her the greater pleasure, may it not have been because she dimly perceived in it a meeting-point between the real and the imaginary? Here was a threshold of the great wonder-world that primitive peoples and children love so well. They are the great mystics, after all. And are they not, perhaps, wise mystics who sit and wonder and worship, satisfied not to understand?

Summer waned and went out, and September came in—September, hot and murky and short of breath, as one ill of heart-failure. Even the prayer-meeting women who had taken up Miss

Mary Ellen's case in strong faith, determined not to let it go, were growing faint of heart under the combined pressure of disappointed hope and the summer's weight. The poor object of their prayers, instead of seeming in any wise improved, grew rather more wan and weary as time wore on. Indeed, she sometimes appeared definitely worse, and would often draw rein in the public road to lift the doll from her lap and discuss her anxieties concerning it with any passing acquaintance, or even on occasion to exult in a fancied improvement.

This was a thing she had never done before the women began to pray, and it took a generous dispensation of faith to enable them to continue steadfast in the face of such discouragement. But, as is sometimes the case, greater faith came from the greater need, and the prayer-meeting grew. In the face of its new and painful phases, as the tragedy took on a fresh sadness, even a few churchly women who had stood aloof at the beginning waived their sectarian differences and came into the meeting. And there were strange confessions sometimes at these gatherings, where it was no uncommon thing for a good sister to relate how, on a certain occasion, she had either "burst out cryin' to keep from laughin'," or "laughed like a heathen jest to keep from cryin'."

The situation was now grown so sad and painful that the doctors called a consultation of neighboring physicians, even bringing for the purpose a "specialist" all the way from the Little Rock Asylum, hoping little, but determined to spare no effort for the bettering of things.

After this last effort and its discouraging result, all hope of recovery seemed gone, and so the good women, when they prayed, despairing of human agency, asked simply for a miracle, reading aloud, for the support of their faith, the stories of marvellous healing as related in the gospels.

It was on a sultry morning, after a night of rain, near the end of September. Old Dr. Jenkins stood behind the showcase in his drug-store dealing out quinine pills and earache drops to the poor country folk and negroes, who, with sallow faces or heads bound up, declared themselves "chillin'" or "painful" while they waited. Patient as cows, they stood in line while the dispensing hand of healing passed over to their tremulous, eager palms the promised "help" for their assorted "miseries."

It was a humble crowd of sufferers, deferring equally, as they waited, to the dignitary who served them and to his environment of mysterious potencies, whose unreadable Latin labels glared at them in every direction as if in challenge to their faith and respect. To the thoughtful observer it seemed an epitome of suffering humanity—patient humanity waiting to be healed by some great and mysterious Unknowable.

It may have been their general attitude of unconscious deference that moved the crowd to fall quickly back at the entrance of the first assertive visitor of the morning, or perhaps old 'Pollo, the negro, as he came rushing into the shop, would have been accorded right of way in a more pretentious gathering. There was certainly that in his appearance which demanded attention.

He had galloped up to the front door, his horse in a lather from the long, hot ride from the Williams homestead, four miles away, and, throwing his reins across the pommel of his saddle, had burst into the drug-store with an excited appeal:

"Doctor Jinkins, come quick! For Gord's sake! Miss Mary Ellen *need* you, Marse Doctor—she need you—*right off!*"

He did not wait for a response. He had delivered his summons, and, turning without another word, he remounted his horse and rode away.

It was not needed that the doctor should offer any apologies to his patients for following him. He did not, indeed, seem to remember that they were there as he seized his coat, and, without even waiting to put it on, quickly unhitched his horse tied at the front door, and followed the negro down the road.

It was a matter of but a few moments to overtake him, and when the two were riding abreast the doctor saw that the old man was crying.

"De dorg, he must 'a' done it, Marse Doctor," he began, between sobs. "He must 'a' got in las' night. It was so hot we lef' all de do's open, same lak we *been* doin'— But it warn't we-alls fault, doctor. But de dorg, he must 'a' snatch de doll out'n de cradle an' run out in de yard wid it, an' it lay a-soakin' in de rain all night. When Miss Mary Ellen fust woked up dis mornin', she called out to Milly to fetch de baby in to her. Milly she often teeks it out'n de cradle early in de mornin' 'fo' missy wakes up, an' make pertend lak she feeds it in de kitchen. An' dis mornin', when she call for it, Milly, she 'spon' back, 'I 'ain't got her, missy!' jes dat-a-way. An' wid dat, 'fo' you could bat yo' eye, missy was hop out'n dat bed an' stan' in de middle o' de kitchen in her night-gownd, white in de face as my whitewash-bresh. An' when she had look at Milly an' den at me, she sclaim out, '*Whar my child?*' I tell you, Marse Doctor, when I see dat look an' heah dat inquiry, I trimbled so dat dat kitchen flo' shuck tell de kittle-leds on de stove rattled. An' Milly, she see how scarified missy look, an' she commence to tu'n roun' an' seek for words, when we heah pit-a-pat, pit-a-pat, on de po'ch; an', good Gord, Marse Doctor! heah come Rover, draggin' dat po' miser'ble little doll-baby in his mouf, drippin' wid mud an' sopped wid rain-water. Quick as I looked at it I see dat bofe eyes was done soaked out an' de paint gone, an' all its yaller hair it had done eve'y bit soaked off. Sir? Oh, I don't know, sir, how she gwine teck it. Dey ain't no sayin' as to dat. She hadn't *come to* when I come away. She had jes drapped down in a dead faint in the mids' o' de kitchen, an' I holp Milly lif' her on to de bed, an' I come for you. Co'se I had to stop an' ketch de horse; an' de roads, dey was so awful muddy an'—"

It was a long ride over the heavy roads, and as the good doctor trotted along, with the old darky steadily talking beside him, he presently ceased to hear.

Having once realized the situation, his professional mind busied itself in speculations as to the probable result of so critical an incident to his patient. Accident, chance, or mayhap a kind providence, had done for her the thing he had long wished to try but had not dared. The mental shock, with the irreparable loss of the doll, would probably have a definite effect for good or ill—if, indeed, she would consent even now to give it up. Of course there was no telling.

This question was almost immediately answered, however, for when, presently, the old negro led the way into the lane leading to the Williams gate, preceding the doctor so as to open the gate for him, he leaned suddenly over his horse's neck and peered eagerly forward. Then drawing rein for a moment, he called back:

"Marse Doctor, look hard, please, sir, an' see what dat my ol' 'oman Milly is doin' out at de front gate."

The doctor's eyes were little better than his companion's. Still, he was able in a moment to reply:

"Why, old man, she is tying a piece of white muslin upon the gate-post. Something has happened."

"White is for babies, ain't it, Marse Doctor?"

"Yes—or for—"

"Den it mus' be she's give it up for dead."

The old man began sobbing again.

"Yes; thank God!" said the doctor. And he wiped his eyes.

The bit of fluttering white that hung upon the gate at the end of the lane had soon told its absurd and pitiful little tale of woe to the few passers-by on the road—its playful announcement of half the story, the comedy side, pathetically suggesting the tragedy that was enacting within.

Before many hours all Simpkinsville knew what had happened, and the little community had succumbed to an attack of hysteria.

Simpkinsville was not usually of a particularly nervous or hysterical temper, but a wholesome sense of the ludicrous, colliding with her maternal love for her afflicted child, could not do less than find relief in simultaneous laughter and tears.

And still, be it said to their credit, when the good women separated, after meeting in the various houses to talk it over, it was the mark of tears that remained upon their faces.

But when it was presently known that their nerve poise was to be critically tested by a "funeral" announced for the next day, there was less emotion exhibited, perhaps, and there were more quiet consultations among the serious-minded.

"'WHITE IS FOR BABIES'"

When Miss Mary Ellen, prostrate and wan with the burden of her long-borne sorrow, had from her pillow quietly given instructions for the burial, the old doctor, who solicitously watched beside her, in the double capacity of friend and physician, had not been able to say her nay.

And when on the next day he had finally invited a conference on the subject with her brother, the minister, his fellow-doctor, and several personal friends of the family, there were heavy lines about his eyes, and he confessed that before daring his advice on so sensitive a point he had "walked the flo' the livelong night."

And then he had strongly, unequivocally, advised the funeral.

"We've thought it best to humor her all the way through," he began, "an' now, when the end is clairly in sight, why, there ain't any consistency in changin' the treatment. Maybe when it's buried she'll forget it, an' in time come to herself. Of co'se it 'll be a tryin' ordeel, but there's enough of us sensible relations an' friends thet 'll go through it, if need be." He had walked up and down the room as he spoke, his hands clasped behind him, and now he stopped before the minister. "Of co'se, Brother Binney"—he spoke with painful hesitation—"of co'se she'll look for you to come an' to put up a prayer, an' maybe read a po'tion o' Scripture. An' I've thought *that* over. Seems to me the whole thing is sad enough for religious services—ef anything is. I've seen reel funerals thet wasn't half so mo'nful, ef I'm any judge of earthly sorrers. There wouldn't be any occasion to bring in the doll in the services, I don't think. But there ain't any earthly grief, in my opinion, but's got a Scripture tex' to match it, ef it's properly selected."

A painful stillness followed this appeal. And then, after closing his eyes for a moment as if in prayer, the good minister said:

"Of course, my dear friends, *you* can see thet this thing can't be conducted *as a funeral*. But, as our good brother has jest remarked, for all the vicissitudes of life—and death—for our safety in joy and our comfort in sorrow, we are given precious words of sweet and blessed consolation."

The saddest funeral gathering in all the annals of Simpkinsville—so it is still always called by those who wept at the obsequies—was that of Miss Mary Ellen's doll, led by the good brother on the following day.

The prayer-meeting women were there, of

course, fortified in their faith by the supreme demand laid upon it, and even equipped with fresh self-control for this crucial test of their poise and worthiness. Their love was deep and sincere, and yet so sensitive were they to the dangers of this most precarious situation that when presently the minister entered, book in hand, a terrible apprehension seized them.

It was as a great wave of indescribable fright, so awful that for a moment their hearts seemed to stop beating, so irresistible in its force that unless it should be quickly stayed it must presently break in some emotion.

No doubt the good brother felt it too, for instead of opening his book, as had been his intention, he laid it down upon the table before him—the small centre-table upon which lay what seemed a tiny mound heaped with flowers—and, placing both hands upon the bowed head of the little woman who sat beside it, closed his eyes, and raised his face heavenward.

"Dear Lord, Thou knowest," he said, slowly. Then finding no other words, perhaps, and willing to be still, he waited a moment in silence.

When he spoke again the wave had broken. The air seemed to sway with the indescribable vibrations that tell of silent weeping, and every face was buried in a handkerchief.

"Thou knowest, O Lord," he resumed, presently, raising his voice a little as if in an access of courage—"Thou knowest how dear to our hearts is Thy handmaiden, this beloved sister who sits in sorrow among us to-day. Thou knowest how we love her. Thou knowest that her afflictions are ours. And oh, dear Father, if it be possible, grant that when we have reverently put this poor little symbol of our common sorrow out of sight forever, Thy peace may descend and fill her heart and ours with Thy everlasting benediction."

The words, which had come slowly, though without apparent effort, might have been inspired. Surely they sounded to the women who waited as if uttered by a voice from Heaven, and to their spiritually attuned ears it was a voice comforting, composing, quieting.

After this followed a reading of Scripture—a selection taken for its wide application to all God's sorrowing people—and the singing of the beautiful hymn,

"God shall charge His angel legions
Watch and ward o'er thee to keep."

This was sung, without a break, from the beginning clear through to the end, with its sweet promise to the grief-stricken of "life beyond the grave." Then came the benediction—the benediction of the churches since the days of the apostles, used of all Christians the world over, but ever beautiful and new—"The peace of God, which passeth all understanding, keep your hearts and minds," etc.

All the company had risen for this—all excepting Miss Mary Ellen, who during the entire ceremony had not changed her position—and when it was finished, when the moment of silent prayers was over and one by one the women rose from their knees, there came an awkward interval pending the next step in this most difficult and exceptional service.

The little woman in whose behalf it had been conducted, for whom all the prayers had been said, made no sign by which her further will should be made known. It had been expected that she would herself go to the burial, and against this contingency a little grave had been prepared in the family burial-ground, which, happily, was situated upon her own ground, in a grove of trees a short distance from the house.

After waiting for some moments, and seeing that she still did not move, the reverend brother finally approached her and laid his palm as before upon her head. Then, quickly reaching around, he drew her hand from beneath her cheek, felt her pulse, and now, turning, he motioned to the doctor to come.

The old man, Dr. Jenkins, lifted her limp arm tenderly and felt her wrist, listened with his ear against her bosom, waited, and listened again—and again. And then, laying back the hand tenderly, he took his handkerchief from his pocket and wiped his eyes.

"Dear friends," he said, huskily, "your prayers have been answered. Sister Mary Ellen has found peace."

THE DIVIDING-FENCE

A SIMPKINSVILLE EPISODE

THE DIVIDING-FENCE

THE widow Carroll and widower Bradfield were next neighbors. Indeed, they were the nearest next neighbors in Simpkinsville, their houses, contrary to the village fashion, standing scarce thirty feet apart.

The cordial friendly relations long existing between the two families were still indicated by the well-worn "stoop" set in the dividing-fence between the two gardens, its three steps on either side a perpetual invitation to social intercourse. Here, in the old days, the two wives were wont to meet for neighborly converse, each generally sitting on her own side, while the "landing" at the stoop's summit answered for table, set conviently between them. Here it had been a common thing to see two thimbles standing off duty beside spools of thread and bits of sewing—little sleeves or patch-work squares—while their mistresses bent over flower beds or pots; for many an industrious intention was thwarted by the witchery of growing things on both sides the fence. Indeed, every one of the fine flowering geraniums that bloomed on either porch had at one time or another passed over this stoop as a cutting, or been taxed in some of its members for the friendly transit.

Here, too, had passed cake receipts and pantalet patterns, bits of yeast-cake and preserving-kettles. Here were exchanged comments upon last Sunday's sermons, and lengthy opinions upon such questions as frequently disturb the maternal mind; as, for instance, whether it were wiser for parents to put their children through the contagious diseases of childhood as opportunity offered, or to shun them, hoping for life-long immunity. In such arguments as this Mrs. Carroll had usually the advantage of a positive opinion. On this identical question, for example, she had frankly declared her sentiments in this wise:

"Well, they's some ketchin' diseases thet I'd send my child'en after in a minute, ef they was handy; an' then, agin, they's others thet I wouldn't dare to, though, ef they *was* to come, I'd be glad when they was over. Any disease thet's got any principle to it I ain't afeerd to tackle, sech ez measles, which they've been measles, behavin' 'cordin' to rule, comin' an' goin' ef they was kep' het an' sweated correct, ever sence the first measle. But scarlet-fever, now, f'instance, that's another thing. My b'lief is thet God sends some diseases, an' the devil, he sends others."

Mrs. Bradfield had agreed that perhaps it *was* a mother's duty to carry her children through as many ailments as possible while she was here to see to it, and yet—for her part—well, she "didn't know." She had known *even measles* to— "But, of co'se, they was black measles, or else they wasn't properly drawed out o' the circulation," she had finally allowed. "And, of co'se, ez you say, Mis' Carroll, maybe they *wasn't* measles. You can't, to say, rightly prove a measle thet ain't broke out. Tell the truth, I'd be fearful to sen' for *any* disease less'n it had a'ready come an' gone 'thout killin' nobody, which would seem to prove thet it wasn't of a fatal nature. An' then, of co'se, it 'd be too late *to* get it. But ez to ascribin' diseases either *up* or *down*, Mis' Carroll," she had concluded, "I wouldn't *dare* do it, less'n I might be unconsciously honorin' the Evil One or *dis*honorin' God."

"An', of co'se," Mrs. Carroll had smilingly replied—"of co'se *I* don't want to give Satan no mo'n his due, neither. But they do say, 'God sends the babies their teeth, and lets the devil set 'em in'—an' that's why the pore little things have sech trouble cuttin' 'em. Seem like the wrastle with Satan begins pretty early. 'Cordin' to that, the Old Boy was, ez you might say, the first dentist, an' all the endurin' dentists sence 'ain't been able to cast him out o' the profession."

"No, an' never will, I reckon, till he is required to hand in his pattern for jaw-teeth roots, *an' to go by it.* But, *bein'* Satan, an' of co'se unprincipled, I reckon he wouldn't keep to it, even then."

Of course in this, as in all next-neighbor friendships, there had been points of contact that could easily have induced friction, but they were never openly confessed, and are certainly now unworthy of more than such casual notice as an unfolding retrospect may reveal.

It was nearly two years now since the two thimbles had rested on the stoop landing. In the interval sorrow had entered both gates. The crêpe band upon Bradfield's Sunday hat was gradually loosening of its own accord, until now every passing breeze seemed to threaten his good wife's memory. But the figure was playing him false, so far as any open manifestation of forgetfulness went.

His neighbor had never worn crêpe, but her

mourning was still in evidence in all its pristine moderation on every important occasion. Simpkinsville conventions were lax as regards this tribute paid her dead, and gauged the loyalty of their surviving relations by other than color standards. A good black alpaca dress in hand needed not even to surrender its bands of velvet, not to mention its lustre, to serve as widow's weeds, a first evidence of its wearer's "beginning to take notice" being perhaps not so much the "Valenceens ruche" which was expected to appear at her neck in due season as that which it ushered in. The new order meant reappearance at church sociables after lamp-light, taking part at fairs and the like, and a final emergence in full feather of forgetfulness at the spring barbecue or camp-meeting.

The widow Carroll, always a woman of her own mind, had *begun* with the Valenciennes ruche, nor had she ever forsaken her post as server of meats at church functions. But during the two years of her mourning she had not changed. There had been no second stage. She had not meant, from the beginning, that there should be. If she should ever marry again, the "good ez new" blue ribbon bow, ripped off her black dress for the funeral, would naïvely reappear in its old place, pinned in the centre with the now discarded coral pin. But this is unprofitable surmise.

Of course Dame Gossip had married her offhand to her neighbor before his wife was decently buried. And of course a woman of Mary Carroll's strength of mind had ignored all such predictions, and had done all the things a less self-reliant woman would not have dared. She had "done for Susan's children jest exactly ez ef they'd been her own sister's, from the start." This tribute even the busy tongues of the village had finally been constrained to accord her.

The situation, like the ruche, though startling at first, had remained as unaltered. The stoop was still, in a different way, as conducive to friendly intercourse as of yore. Though the maternal neighbor had never crossed it, excepting twice, in cases of sickness, she had not hesitated to utilize it as a dispensing-station for sundry neighborly ministrations, as when on raw mornings "in-the-spring-o'-the-year," after similarly fortifying her own brood, she had armed herself with quinine capsules and a gourd dipper of water, and administered the bitter refreshment to the entire Bradfield lot, even on one occasion including the *pater*. Nor had she stopped at this; for, after the passage of the friendly swallow, she was heard to observe, in all seriousness, "Mr. Bradfield, I see they's a fillin' done come out o' one o' yore back teeth, an' I'd advise you to look after it." And then, her errand fully accomplished, she had turned back to her own house. It was not her habit to linger about the stoop for idle parley. Needless to say, Bradfield rode out to consult the dentist that day.

The situation thus briefly sketched seemed, indeed, to have reached a state of entire safety, as far as any possible romance was concerned. But how often are apparent safety-lines found to be charged with strong and dangerous currents! Strange to say, it was just when gossip had declared against its early predictions, and was beginning to cast about among its maturer marriageable maidens for the needed "mother for Susan Bradfield's child'en," that Bradfield himself had first reflected with perfected certitude: "The hole in my heart is there yet—jest ez big an' ez holler ez the day pore Susan was buried—an' the only livin' woman thet can ever fill it *to overflowin'* is Mis' Carroll. She knowed Susan an' Susan's ways—an' Susan's child'en. An' she knows me." So the reflection proceeded. "Yas, an' she knows me—*maybe she knows me too well.* Ef they's any trouble, it 'll be that."

The years of intimate friendship had not

passed, indeed, without Bradfield's realizing that certain qualities in himself had fallen under the ban of Mrs. Carroll's disapproval. True, he and she had been as different persons then, and yet, after all, they were the same. The widow Carroll, albeit she was thirty-seven years old, and "the mother o' five," was a pretty woman. She was one of those pretty women who, though never threatened with great beauty, being made on too chubby a pattern, seem to possess in healthy fulness all the womanly charms incident to every passing stage in life. She was a flower always in process of bloom — a woman of dimples, but whose dimples went to grace a smile or dissipate a frown rather than to count as dimples, mere physical incidents. Her crisp hair, a coppery auburn in hue, commonly called red, was full of fine lights and color—such hair as is at once the glory and the despair of the village poet, who recklessly uses up *shimmer* and *glimmer* in a first couplet, only to be confronted with *gleam* and *sheen*, that, with fair promise of affiliation, stubbornly refuse to lend themselves to his poetic scheme. There is the red hair that smiles, and the red hair that scolds and is capable of profanity. One kind reflects light and warmth, the other burns. Mary Carroll's was of the smiling sort.

Although Bradfield had felt the radiant glory of the widow's head as he often viewed it in the morning sun from his side of the fence, and had more than once compared it to her shining copper kettle inverted on the shed, to the disadvantage of the gleaming metal, he had summarily denounced such thoughts not only as unbecoming his crêpe, but as being of a nature "to nachelly disgust sech a sensible mother o' child'en ez Mis' Carroll, ef she'd even s'picioned sech a thing."

Just how or when Bradfield had finally declared his mind not even the writer of these annals professes to know. But there is evidence that the arguments which elicited the following somewhat lengthy response from the widow were not his first words on the subject. Bradfield was standing on his side the fence down in the rear garden: Mrs. Carroll on her side.

"Yas," she spoke with hesitation—"yas, I know it's jest ez you say, Mr. Bradfield. The best pickets in this dividin'-fence 'd be a-plenty to patch up the outside fences of both our yards with; an' one o' the two front gates *could* be took out an' put in where the back gate on my side is rotted out; an' ez you say, one kitchen an' one cook 'd do where it takes two now, an'—an' of co'se our houses do set so close-t together thet we could easy, *ez you say,* jest roof over the space between 'em an' make it into a good wide hall, an'—an' of co'se our child'en do, ez you say, ez good ez live together ez it is, an'—but—" She knit her brow and hesitated.

"*And* is a heap purtier word 'n what *but* is, Mis' Carroll."

Bradfield chuckled nervously as he leaned forward towards her, his elbows resting upon the ledge of the dividing-fence between them as he spoke.

The widow laughed. "Yas, I know it is, but—" She colored. "I declare, I didn't lay out to say *but* so soon again, but— Well, I *do* declare!"

And now both laughed.

"Did it ever strike you, Mis' Carroll," Bradfield resumed, presently—"did it ever strike you ez funny thet whoever planted them trees down yo' front walk an' down mine should o' been so opposite *an'* similar minded ez to set a row o' silver-poplars down the lef' side o' my walk an' down the right side o' yoze, so's ef we *was* ever minded to cut out the middle rows o' arbor-vitæs and cedars (which are too much alike an' too different to agree side by side anyway), we could have a broad av'nue o' silver-poplars clean down f'om the house to the front gate? See?" He pointed first to the space between the two houses, and then to the fence. "Of co'se, the new po'ch, now, it 'd projec' out in the middle-centre o' the av'nue, too. An' I was thinkin' it 'd be purty, maybe, to have a high cornish 'round it, like that 'n on the new school-house, on'y higher an' mo' notched, ef you say so. An' the drive up the av'nue, it could be laid either in shell or brick, jest ez you say—or maybe gravel. Why, it looks to me ez ef, ef we *was* to th'ow the two houses into one that-a-way, we'd have what I'd call *a res-i-dence*—that's what we would. An' the money we'd save in a year, j'inin' the two households, 'd pay for the improvements, too."

"Yas, I reckon 'twould, Mr. Bradfield, ef 'twas handled economical. I reckon 'twould—but— Ain't that a yaller tomater down there in yo' tomater-patch? I didn't know you planted yallers."

"No, I haven't. That there's a squash flower, I vow, with two bees in it this minute. Them simlins 're nachel gadders. The root o' that 'n is clair 'crost the walk. They don't no mo' hesitate to go where they ain't invited an' to lay their young ones in the laps of anything thet 'll hold 'em than—"

"Than some folks do, I reckon."

Bradfield's eyes searched her face suspiciously. "Ma-am?" The word was long drawn out.

"No insinuation intended, Mr. Bradfield, of co'se. I was only thinkin' o' the way Sally Ann Brooks sends her young ones roun' town to spen' the day to get shet of 'em, 'stid of—"

"Oh, I see! Reckon I'll plant bush-squash myself after this. I don't want nothin' meanderin' roun' my garden thet makes sech a pore figger o' speech ez a simlin do. Th' ain't nothin' too low down an' common for 'em to mix with ef they git a half a chance, f'om a punkin even down to a dipper-gourd. An' I wouldn't trust 'em too near a wash-rag vine an' leave off watchin' 'em, they're that p'omiscuyus-minded."

"I s'pose, Mr. Bradfield, the bush-squash does live, ez Elder Billins says, a mo' virtuous life, stayin' home an' jest having a lapful o' reg'lar young bush-squashes, every one saucer-shaped an' scalloped 'roun' the edges, same ez all respectable Christian families should do. An' talkin' o' squashes, I'd say thet maybe Elder Billins was right when he remarked thet bush-squashes was mo' femi*nine*-minded 'n what runners was."

"Well," Bradfield chuckled, "I'll promise you, ef you'll say the word, to take down this useless fence, they sha'n't be a runnin'-squash allowed inside *our garden.*"

"Th' ain't no hurry about that, I reckon, Mr. Bradfield," she answered, playfully. "An' I mus' be goin' up to the house now. I jest stepped down to see ef my yallers was colorin'. I'm goin' to start preservin' to-morrer. Better send yore Tom over an' let me look at his throat again to-day. You see, he can't gargle, an' it's jest ez well to ward off so'e throat for sech child'en. Good-mornin', Mr. Bradfield."

Instead of answering, Bradfield followed beside her on his side the fence.

"An' *I* come down here, Mis' Carroll," he resumed, directly — "I come down, *seein' you here,* and hopin' maybe to dis-cuss things a little. This dividin'-fence, now; it's made out o' good-heart lumber, every picket an' post, an' our outside pickets 're worm-et tur'ble—both yoze an' mine. Ef we could jest to say th'ow these two garden patches into one— I've got a good sparrer-grass bed on my side, ez you see, an' you're jest a-*proj*ec'in' to start another one, which you needn't do; an' yore butter-bean arbor is ez stiddy ez the day it was put up, an' mine is about ez ramshackled ez they get; an' both the sparrer-grass bed *an'* the arbor 're big enough for the two families—or for one, I mean—twice-t ez big ez either, which ours would pre-cize-ly bė. Since it's took possession of my mind, Mis' Carroll, it's astonishin' how the surpluses on one side o' the fence do seem to match the lacks on the other. An' the fence *itself*, for *it* to be so well worth takin' down, why, it looks to me like flyin' in the face o' Prov-i-dence to hold out against so many hints *to* do a special thing."

"Well, maybe it is, Mr. Bradfield, but I haven't been given the clair sight to see it that-a-way—yet. The way *I* look at it, that fence is strong enough to do good service *where it is* for some time to come. You see, it 'd take a mighty wide oil-cloth to cover that middle hall you're a-*proj*ec'in' to let in 'twixt the two houses —an' a front hall 'thout oil-cloth I *wouldn't* have —noway. But maybe I'm worldly minded."

"Cert'n'y not. Oil-cloth pays for itself over an' over ag'in ef it's kep' rubbed up an' varnished occasional. We might get some o' the drummers to fetch us some samples, jest to look over."

The widow laughed. "Yas, I can see either you or me lookin' over any house-furnishin' samples, now! Why, Simpkinsville wouldn't hold the talk. I do declare ef there ain't Elder Billins a-comin' this way 'crost my yard now, ez I live! How did he manage to tie up 'thout me seein' 'im, I wonder? Did you see 'im stop?"

"Yas, I did—an' befo' I saw 'im I felt 'im. I knowed *somebody* was comin' to pester my sight, an' I wondered who it was befo' he come into the road. I don't know how it is, but they's somethin' in the way a ol' bachelor carries 'isself thet tantalizes me, 'special when I see 'im try to wait on a woman thet can't see 'im ez *re*dic'lous ez I see 'im. A ol', dried-up, singular number, mascu*line* gender don't know no mo' what 'll tickle a woman's fancy 'n one o' them sca'crows in my pea-patch out yonder. An' yet they 'ain't got the settled mind thet a sca'crow has—to stay peaceable in that station of life unto which it has pleased God to call 'em."

The widow laughed merrily. "You better hursh, Mr. Bradfield. Elder Billins may be slow some ways, but his ears don't set out the way they do for nothin'. What's that he's a-fetchin'?"

"Don't know ez I know exac'ly. I see he *is* loaded up."

"I wonder for goodness' sakes, what he's a-fetchin'?

"Howdy, Elder!" she called out cheerily now. "Come right along! I won't go to meet you, 'cause I know you an' Mr. Bradfield 'll want to shake hands over the fence." She cast a mischievous glance at Bradfield as she advanced a single step towards Billins.

"Excuse my hands, please, Elder. Tyin' up them soggy tomater bushes has greened 'em so th' ain't fit *to* offer you—but *howdy!* Ef he ain't gone an' done it, *spite* of me! Made me another perfec'ly lovely hangin'-basket!" Her eyes beamed as a child's over a new toy as Billins set a tall rustic structure down before her.

"Jest look, Mr. Bradfield," she continued, raising it for inspection. "I *do* declare, Elder, how you manage to twis' these roots in an' out I don't know. 'Tain't made on the same plan ez the chair, either. That chair you set in, Mr. Bradfield, the other day when you come up on my po'ch to fetch the onion sets, Elder Billins made me that; an' for a chair to ease a tired back, or jest to set in an' study braidin' patterns, it's the most accommodatin' chair a person ever did set in. Mr. Bradfield said *'isself*, Elder, thet he never *had* set in a chair thet yielded to his needs like it did."

"But I was figgerin' on a man's idee of a easy-settin' chair," Bradfield retorted. "I'd o' thought you'd 'a' made a lady a cushioned chair, Billins, with side-rockers to it, an' maybe a movable foot-rest, or even a tune-playin' seat in it."

"So I would ef she'd a-said the word, but when a lady says rustics, it's rustics to me, ef I have to dig up all the crooked roots in the county."

The discussion of the rustic basket had so engaged their attention that the men seemed to have forgotten a formal greeting, but now, when the widow presented her own hand a second time to Billins, thanking him for his gift, by the faintest movement of the wrist and an inclination of the head towards the fence, she virtually passed him over to Bradfield.

"Howdy, Eben! Hope I see you well." Billins heartily extended his hand quite over the fence.

Bradfield had never heard of the fashionable lofty salutation in mid-air, but it was with precisely this inane shoulder-high denial of cordiality that he changed the friendly impulse of the proffered hand from a hearty downward shake to a quick lateral movement quite even with the top of the pickets.

"I'm toler'ble peart, thanky, Elder," he drawled. "How's yoreself? You seem to be renewin' yo' youth like the eagle."

"Well, Eben, ef you count yo'self a eagle, I ain't perpared to dispute that," was the Elder's humorous reply. And then he added, more seriously, "How's the lambs, Eben?"

"The kids? Oh, they're purty toler'ble frisky, thanky. Reckon to sech ez you they'd seem mo' like roa'in' lions 'n lambs. They do say thet folks thet roam single all their lives forgits they ever was kids theirselves."

"Well, Eben, sence you mention it, I reckon sech of us ez are strivin' to stand with the *sheep* at the jedgment 'd ruther take their chances *startin'* ez a *lamb*. Ef a person starts out ez a *kid*, seem to *me* the best he can *hope* to do 'd be to grow into a *goat*, which is classed ez purty pore cattle both here *an'* hereafter. Yore dear child'en 're *lambs*, Eben—lambs o' the Lord's fold, an' I hate to hear you mis-designate 'em that-a-way."

Elder Billins spoke with the religious voice—the same that was wont to say on frequent occasion, "Brother Bradfield, won't you lead in prayer?" Bradfield had often led in prayer by its mild invitation, and he recognized it as a force commanding respect. For a moment, under its benign influence, he was somewhat mollified, and was opening his lips for such conciliatory speech as he could command, when Billins remarked, with an insinuating smile:

"I s'pose you an' Mis' Carroll 've been swappin' confi*den*ces about garden-truck this heavenly mornin'. You seem to have the first flower on yo' side, Eben. I see some sort o' blossom down behind you there."

"Yas; th' ain't much inter*est*in' in the gardens yet. That one flower with a couple o' bees a-buzzin' round it is about the only, to say, inter*est*in' thing in sight—that is to say, for beauty."

Billins chuckled. "Well, I declare, Eben Bradfield, seem to me you described more'n you set out to describe that time. Ef my eyes don't deceive me, I see a-*nother* flower with two more bees a-buzzin' round it." He glanced at the widow, and then at Bradfield.

"Don't know ez I see that, Elder—eggsac'ly—that is, ez to the bees."

"You don't, don't you? Spell Bradfield, an' then spell Billins. Oho! You see it now, don't you? Ef we ain't two B's, what 'd you say we was?"

Bradfield cleared his throat. "Seem to me, Elder, I'd be purty hard pushed for com-pliments 'fore I'd compare a lady to a squash flower."

"Well, Eben, that ain't exac'ly my fault, the way I look at it. I supplied the com-pli-ment, an' you supplied the flower. I jest took the best you had, which, it seems to me, is the brightest thing on the face o' the lan'scape—

exceptin', of co'se—" He lifted his hat and bowed to the widow.

Bradfield colored up to the roots of his hair as he said, smiling defiantly: "Them wasn't stingin'-bees around that simlin flower, Elder. They was jest these innercent white-faced buzzers. Look out thet you don't spile yo' figger o' speech by strikin' too hard. That's the second stroke o' el-o-quence thet's been struck off from that one flower to-day, an' I've had to dodge both times, seem like. Reckon I'll dodge now, shore enough, an' bid you both good-mornin'. Elder didn't come to pay me a visit, noways, an' I think I know when three's a crowd." And Bradfield, as fretful as a spoiled boy, turned across his own garden and left them.

"Well, I must say, I'm dis-gust-ed!" he said, audibly, as soon as he dared. "*More*'n dis-gusted! It's enough to make a person sick to his stummick! The idee of a ol' white-haired exhorter like Elder Billins whisperin' that he'd wove her name into a rustic basket with a motter throwed in! Seem like she'd o' laughed right out in his face. Lordy, but it's *that* sickenin'! I do thank the Lord I'm a perfessin' Christian or *I'd swear—dog-gone* ef I wouldn't!"

When he had reached his own porch, Bradfield drew a chair to its remote end and sat down. "The idee!" he exclaimed as he balanced his body back against the wall, extending his feet over the banisters. "The idee o' him havin' mo' cheek 'n what I've got! Here I 'ain't dared to more 'n broach things in a business way, an', shore's I'm alive, that ol' bone 's a-courtin' 'er outspoken."

And now, in a fashion entirely at variance with his late expressions, Bradfield's secret thoughts took shape. "Wonder ef any other woman ever did have sech a head, anyhow? The way them curls snug up to her neck—Lordy, but it all but takes my breath away. An' as for *tac'—an'* cleverness—well, they never was sech another woman, I know. Ef she 's'picioned what a blame ejiot I am about her, she wouldn't have no mo' respec' for me 'n nothin'. But I know how to tackle 'er, that I do! She's a reg'lar business thorough-goer, she is, an' the man thet gets her, he's got to prove the common-sense o' the thing—that's what he's got to do. The idee o' hangin'-baskets an' motters to a person o' her sense—an' she the mother o' five! Don't b'lieve I ever seen 'er yet—*at home*—'thout a bunch o' keys hangin' to 'er belt, or a thimble on; an' ez to aprons— To me a apron is a thing thet sets off a purty woman, an' jest nachelly dis-figgers a ugly one—not to mention her dis-figgerin' it."

He chuckled, drew down his feet, and began walking up and down his porch. "The idee o' me ca'culatin' *to a cent* what we could save by j'inin' interests, an', come down to the truth, I'd spend the last cent I've got to get 'er. But she mustn't know it. Oh no, she mustn't know it."

Pausing here at the end of the porch, he cast his eyes down towards the rear lot, taking in in his survey a view of both gardens. "Wonder where those child'en o' mine have went to?" he continued, mentally. "Over in her barn, I'll venture, the last one of 'em, playin' with hers, 'ceptin' her Joe, an' I'll lay he's with my Tom, sailin' shingle boats down in my goose-pond.

"'Tis funny, come to think of it, for me to have a goose-pond an' for her to have the geese. We ain't to say duplicated on nothin', 'less 'n 'tis child'en, an' we're so pre-cize-ly matched in them thet—well, it's comical, that's what it is. Reckon, after we was married awhile, they 'd come so nachel thet, takin' 'em hit an' miss, we wouldn't know no diff'rence hardly. *One thing shore*, the day she gives her solemn consent to mother mine, I'll start a-fatherin' hers jest ez conscientious ez I know how."

He resumed his promenade, his irregular step

keeping pace with his musings. "I never have gone over to set of a evening yet. I would 'a' went sev'al nights, but I'm 'feerd she might th'ow out hints about motherless child'en lef' to their devious ways, or some other Scriptu'al insinuation. S'pose I'd *haf* to say at home where I was goin'. Ef I didn't, *hers* would tell *mine* first thing nex' mornin'. I would 'a' went in to set awhile Sunday night when we walked home f'om church, ef she'd 'a'—well, maybe it would o' seemed too pointed to ask me. It's true I did have my little Mamie asleep 'crost my shoulder, but I could 'a' laid her on the parlor sofy till I'd got ready to go home. Strange how that baby o' mine has took sech a notion to go to church—an' drops off to sleep du'in' the first prayer every time. Ef it was anywhere else I mightn't humor her. Somehow, a baby sleepin' on a person's shoulder is a hind'rance to a person—in some things. But of co'se any signs of early piety should be encouraged, though I doubt how much o' the gospel she gets—at three—'pecial when she's sno'ein'. There goes ol' Billins now—at last—pore ol' ejiot thet he is! Ef he didn't disgust me so I'd laugh right out."

If the widow bore about with her any consciousness of the strictly business-like romance that was throwing its tendrils over the dividing-fence between her home and her neighbor's—a romance as devoid of visible leaf or blossom as the vermicelli-like love-vine that spread its yellow tangle over certain vine-clad sections of it—she gave no sign of such consciousness by the slightest deviation from her ordinary routine.

Nothing was forgotten in her well-ordered household, though a close observer might have suspected a sort of fierce thoroughness in all she did. It was only after the children were all snugly put to bed that night that she took one from the row of daguerreotypes which stood open upon her high parlor mantel, and, bringing it to her bedroom lamp, scanned it closely.

"Funny to think how a man can change so," she said, audibly, as if addressing the picture, which she turned from side to side, viewing it at one angle and another. "When Eben Bradfield an' Susan had this picture took they wasn't a more generous-handed husband in the State 'n what he was. Susan paid five dollars to have her hair braided that-a-way while she was down in New 'Leans, a hundred and fifty plat'. An' Eben was tickled to have her pay it, too. She had this limpy flat hair thet all runs to len'th an' ain't fittin' for nothin' else but *to* braid. An' that black polonay she's got on, it was fo' dollars a yard; 'n' he bought her that gold tasselled watch-chain that trip too, an' them fingered mits. An' they sat in whole plush curtained off sections at the theatre, too, an' boa'ded at the St. Charles Hotel at fo' dollars a day apiece. So they bragged when they come home. I never *did* see such a waste o' money, an' I didn't hesitate to say so, neither. It used to do me good them days to give her an' Eben a 'casional rap over the knuckles for their extravagance. Pore Susan was beginnin' to look mighty peaked an' consumpted, even in this picture. Death was on 'er then, I reckon."

Hesitating here, she wiped the face of the picture and studied it in silence, but her thoughts fairly flew, as she thus mentally reviewed the situation:

"But to think of Eben Bradfield spendin' money like water the way he done for Susan, an' I knowin' it—*an' he knowin' I know it*—an' then layin' off to stint me the way he does!

"I don't doubt he *spoke* the word to save paper an' ink. Eben is a handsome man, even here, with his hen-pecked face an' chin whiskers on, an' I *used* to think he was a good one, an' I won't say he ain't; but he is shorely changed—

sadly changed. Du'in' the month thet he's showed signs o' keepin' comp'ny with me—which he has ac*chilly* asked me to marry him—he 'ain't said the first word sech ez you'd expect of a co'tin' widower, *exceptin' one.* The day he remarked thet he felt ez young ez he ever did, thinks I to myself, 'Now you're comin' *to!*' An' I fully expected the nex' word to be accordin' to that beginnin'. But 'stid o' that, what does he say but 'Yore Rosie's outgrowed dresses 'd come in handy for my Emma, don't you reckon? She's jest about a hem or a couple o' tucks taller 'n what Emma is.' I do declare, Eben Bradfield, lookin' at you here in this picture standin' behind Susan's chair, an' rememberin' how you squandered money on her, I feel *that disgusted!* Ef it was anybody thet I had less respec' for, I wouldn't care.

"Well, th' ain't no use losin' sleep over a man's meanness, an' it's ten o'clock now," she continued audibly, as she closed the picture with a snap and began taking down her hair, and as she deftly manipulated the shimmering braids, her thoughts turned inward upon herself. "Looks like ez ef a woman *oughtn't* to be lonesome with a houseful o' child'en sech ez I've got," so the introspection began, "an' I *wasn't* lonesome tell Eben Bradfield set me to thinkin'. Ef lonely people could only keep clair o' thinkin', they'd do very well. But I *do* think a man with a whole lot o' growin' child'en on his hands is a pitiful sight. 'Twasn't never intended. I reckon it's a funny thing for me to say, even to myself, but ef I had all the child'en under one roof they'd be less care to me 'n what they are now—*not thet I'd marry that close-fisted Eben Bradfield—to save his life!* But th' ain't a night thet I put mine to bed but I wonder how his are gettin' on — maybe po' little Mamie an' Sudie gettin' their nigh'-gownds hind part befo' or mixed—Mamie treadin' on hers, an' Sudie's up to her knees—an' like ez not hangin' open at the neck. Susan always did work her button-holes too big for her buttons. Some women 're constitutionally that-a-way by nature. Of co'se I couldn't never fall in love again. It 'd be childish. But ef Eben Bradfield was *half* like he used to be, an' ef he cared *a quarter* ez much for me ez Elder Billins does, I'd let him *take* down that dividin'-fence in a minute, an' do my best for Susan's child'en.

"The *first* thing I'd do 'd be to shorten their dress waists. Pore little Sudie! I've seen her set down sudden an' set *clair over the belt,* an' not be able to rise. An' she left 'em *so many,* an' 'lowed for *so much* growth! They never will wear out. Sometimes I think that's one reason her child'en don't grow faster 'n they do. Jest one sight o' them big clo'es is enough to discourage a child out of its growth.

"It's funny—the spite Eben seems to have against Elder Billins. Maybe he reelizes thet Elder is mo' gifted in speech 'n what he is. Ef I ever *should* make up my mind to marry Elder Billins it 'd be a edjucation to my child'en, jest a-livin' with 'im an' hearin' 'im strike off figgers o' speech off-hand. Ef he jest wouldn't slit his boots over his bunions! It's a little thing, but—

"An' then, somehow, I don't know ez I care for a prayer-meetin' voice for all purposes. But, of co'se, hearin' it all the time might encourage my child'en to lead religious lives. I reckon the truth is it 'd be mo' to my child'en's interests to think about marryin' Elder Billins, an' mo' for pore Susan's child'en's good ef I was to take Eben; an' yet—"

And then she added aloud, with a yawn, as she turned out the lamp.

"Well, it's good I don't haf to decide tonight."

THE MIDDLE HALL

A SEQUEL TO "THE DIVIDING-FENCE"

THE MIDDLE HALL

THE dividing-fence was all in bloom. Lady-bank roses overlapped honeysuckle vines over long sections of its rough-hewn pickets, while woodbine and clematis locked arms for the passage of the amorous love-vine, that lay its yellow rings in tangled masses here and there according to its own sweet will.

The atmosphere was teeming with the odors of romance, musical with its small noises. Pollen-dusted bees and yellow-bellied moths — those most irresponsible fathers of hybrid blooms and remote floral kinships—flitted about in the sun-shine, passed and repassed in mid-air by their rival match-makers, the iridescent humming-birds. And there were nests—real birds'-nests—in the vines that clambered on both verandas, the widow Carroll's and that of her neighbor, the widower Bradfield. And from one porch to the other flitted bee and bird and moth, stopping for a sip or a brief wing-rest on the vine-clad fence, while the flowers on either side responded to their amenities in answering hues and friendly conformity.

It was late in the summer afternoon, and the evening twitterings were setting in in a lively chorus, which, to the casual listener, was quite drowned by the voices of children who played "tag" or "prisoners' base" down in the front yards, passing at will from one to the other by certain loose pickets hidden among the vines, known to the small-fry of both families.

Bradfield sat alone upon his porch in the shadows of the foliage, but though he was listening he heard none of these noises of nature. The truth was, Bradfield was listening, albeit with no eavesdropping intention, to a scarcely perceptible hum of voices in the corner of his neighbor's porch. The widow had "company," and the voice that came to Bradfield, alternating with hers, was one he knew.

Elder Billins was now a regular visitor at the widow's home, always presenting himself with a flourish, with the avowed intention of paying a formal visit — a thing Bradfield had not yet found courage to do. He had felt sometimes that if he could just get out of sight of her house to "get a start," he might "make a break for her gate," and go in. Indeed, he did once try this, and found such momentum in the experiment that he had really passed his own gate, and would have entered hers, had not the whole drove of children swooped down upon him with the inquiry, "Where you goin'? Where you goin', pop?" to which he had quickly replied: "Oh, no place! Where *was* I goin', shore enough?" And so he had turned back, only to meet Billins riding up to the widow's gate with a great bouquet of flowers in his hand.

Bradfield wouldn't have been caught offering her a leaf or flower for anything in the world, unless, indeed, it were such a matter as a bunch of alder flowers, a sprig of mint, or a bunch of mullein, for medicinal uses.

No one knew what Mrs. Carroll's attitude towards Billins was, but everybody laughed at him, and of course there were those who blamed her for accepting his attentions, unless, indeed, she intended to marry him—a thing that such as knew her best were morally certain she would never do.

"Mary Carroll jest can't help likin' to have men a-hangin' 'round 'er, no more'n any other woman o' her colored hair can help it," was the verdict, compounded equally of apology and censure, by such of her friends as were managing to worry along through life fairly well without such accessories. But, of course, they had "other colored hair"!

If Mrs. Carroll's main pleasure in Billins's devotion was in its putting Bradfield's prosaic courtship to shame, she never told it.

On the evening with which this chapter opens we have seen that the situation was typical of the real condition of things—Bradfield alone on his porch, cogitating, moody; Billins talking with the widow on hers, full of words and bombast; the children of both houses playing, within range of her vision, from one yard to the other.

Up to this time Bradfield had had the satisfaction of knowing that although Billins was a regular visitor, he had experienced rather "hard luck" in having scarcely a word alone with his hostess.

The truth was that Billins, who was their Sunday-school superintendent, was a great favorite with the children, and when on his presenting himself the little Carrolls and Bradfields would come and, drawing up chairs, seat themselves with modest company manners before him, he could not do less than treat them cordially; and, indeed, more than once the entire lot had monopolized his visit wholly, dutifully volunteering to recite to him their "golden texts," catechism, or selected hymns for the following Sunday's lesson. And for different reasons neither family was ever privately reproved by its respective parent for this artless intrusion.

The widow rather dreaded the unequivocal proposal of marriage which she knew was imminent, as it would end the affair; and she felt that Bradfield needed that it should continue, "under his very eyes," for the present at least.

Bradfield, on his part, was simply glad, on general principles, to thwart Billins's designs, and, indeed, he was guilty of a little indirect manœuvring to this end, as when, on several occasions, he took pains to charge his children to "always ac' nice an' polite to Elder; to ricollec' thet he was their Sund'y-school sup'intendent, which was the same ez a shepherd, an' of co'se he took a heap o' int'rest in all the lambs of 'is flock."

The little Bradfields were gentle of nature, and took readily to hints of politeness; and when they brought their catechisms to Billins for recitation, while little Sudie shared his entire visit, sitting upon his knee, there was no one to chide them for excess of cordiality.

As Bradfield sat listening to the low murmur of voices, with an occasional merry note of laughter from the widow, or a rise in eloquent fervor from Billins, he was most uncomfortable, and was several times tempted to call the children in "out o' the fallin' dew." But it was difficult to do this, for two reasons. First, because he feared that if he should do so the whole crowd would come over to his side, leaving Billins master of the situation, and if he waited a little while Mrs. Carroll would surely call them. And, besides, it would seem almost like an imputation against her watchfulness, for it was she who always decided such matters, and why should he assume that she had forgotten to-night?

But it was growing late, and she did not call them, and Billins's voice was sinking ominously lower. It was well that Bradfield could not hear what he was saying.

To do Eben Bradfield full justice, had this been possible he would have changed his seat—or he thought he would. All honest men think they would flee from such temptation, but there are thousands of estimable men, and women too, who wouldn't do it; for of all negative crimes the simple acceptance of an accidental, unsought advantage is perhaps the most insidious. But Bradfield could not hear a word. He got the form of the conversation, though, and its punctuation reached him in short outbursts of laughter from the widow. But this had not come for some time now. Indeed, Billins's long periods were proclaiming the affair in hand no laughing matter.

Perhaps the last hour of the interview is worth recording here.

"Why," he was saying, when it was quite dark, and Bradfield had for a half-hour thought it time for him to be gone—"why, Mis' Carroll, this thing come to me ez a rev'lation from Heaven—that's what it did. It come to me ez a rev'lation on a most solemn occasion, too. In fact, to show you *how* solemn it was, which nobody reelized more'n what you did, why, it was the day o' yore funeral, Mis' Carroll."

"My funeral, Elder!" She laughed here a little nervously; and Bradfield, suddenly angered, moved his chair to the other end of the porch. "My funeral, Elder! Why, I ain't dead yet, *I hope!*"

"Nor will be for many happy years to come, let us pray, you dear heart! I mean the funeral you *give*, Mis' Carroll—not mentionin' no names."

"Oh!" she gasped.

"Yas; an' you didn't give him no mean one neither; and ef you don't mind me sayin' it, why, I'll tell you what Jim Creese says. Says he, talkin' about that funeral, '*There's* a woman,' says he, 'thet when she pays respects, why, she pays 'em,' says he—jest so. 'Diff'rent fam'lies under affliction had negotiated with me for that sample coffin,' says he, 'but when it come to the price, why, they'd always seem to think maybe 'twasn't right for Christians, believin' in the resurrection o' the dead, to imprison theirs in a metallic—like ez ef when called to appear they couldn't rise an' drop off the coffin same ez a overcoat no longer needed — an' so,' says he, 'they'd fall back on white pine an' satin ribbons, black, white, or mixed, accordin' to age and conditions. But Mis' Carroll, when it come to the worst, why, she jest simply ordered the sample off-hand,' says he, 'never pricin' it nor nothin'.'

"An' now he's done bought a new sample, with side an' top merrors in it, an' he says he's a-waitin' to see the next one dyin' in Simpkinsville thet 'll be thought enough of to lay in it. Have you saw the new sample down in the show-window, Mis' Carroll?"

"No, Elder, I haven't. Tell the truth, I always go round the other way ruther than pass there."

"Well, you'd ought to see it. Th' 'ain't been nothin' like it in these parts before. It cert'n'y is gorgeous, though I can't say ez it attracts me much. I don't see no good in seemin' to be buryin' three, which these merrors reflec'; *and four with the cover on;* though of co'se the fo'th one is only for the benefit o' the occupant. Of co'se some survivers might take comfort in multiplyin' their griefs that-a-way; an' for a departed bachelor or a maiden lady it might relieve the monotony a little, an' make 'em seem more like fam'ly persons, an', after a lonely life, they might care to have sech reflections cast, though *I* wouldn't.

"But that ain't neither here nor there. What I was a-startin' to say was thet it was the day o' this solemn occasion, when we was in the church, an' John Carroll was layin' his last lay in the sample before the pul-pit, when you an' yores had follered him, two by two, up the middle aisle, thet the rev'lation come to me. A voice said in my ear, jest ez plain ez I'm a-sayin' it to you now, 'David Billins,' says it, 'bide yore time in patience, but *there's yore family.'*

"You know, Mis' Carroll," he continued, after a pause, which she did not break, "the tie betwixt John Carroll an' me was mighty close-t. We wasn't no ord'nary friends; an', tell the truth, ef you hadn't a-ordered that sample, why, it was my intention to do it, jest out of respects to the best friend I ever had, which was John hisself, ez you well know. John done everything for me thet a friend could well do in life—an' in death too, ef you give yore consents."

Mrs. Carroll fanned nervously, and found it necessary to move her chair, her quick motion having caught one of its rockers under the banisters. But Billins went on without interruption.

"An' the fact is *I've* did *John* sev'al friendly favors, an' whether you suspicioned it or not, *one* of 'em was keepin' out o' yore way jest ez soon ez I'd saw what his sentiments was to'ards you—long years ago.

"Yes, ez school-girl, maid, wife, *an'* widder, you've always been the first lady o' the republic to David Billins. But John Carroll was my friend, an' sech was, *and is,* my idees o' friendship.

"When I had give you up to him it was like ez ef I had surrendered the last thing on earth; but I give it freely, never expectin' to get it back; an' now its jest ez ef John had sat up in his grave an' said to me: 'Here's your loand, Dave Billins. Take it back—*with interest.*'

"Of co'se they'se some folks thet 'd contend thet under sech circumstances I couldn't *take* no interest in John's child'en; but to my mind —ef you'll excuse me makin' a mighty triflin' figgur o' speech—to *my* mind this is a case where the cheerful takin' of interest on a loand is a proof of friendship.

"An' no jokin', Mis' Carroll, they're about ez handsome a lot o' step-child'en ez any man ever aspired to; an' I don't begrudge it to 'em, neither, not even sech o' their features ez they taken after John. Of co'se yore child'en couldn't be no ways *but* purty, don't keer who fathered 'em; an' John wasn't a bad-lookin' man, neither, though I have thought thet ef looks had a-been all, I might o' stood my chances with John—of co'se I mean befo' I'd fell away like I have. Sence I've started a-thinnin' out, flesh *an'* hair, of co'se I don't claim much ez to looks; but I depend mo' upon yore ricollection o' what I *have been* in my day an' generation to show what conditions I could return to, in part at least, ef home an' happiness an' wife an' child'en should suddenly descend from heaven upon me. Why, I'm jest ez shore thet I'd fatten up under it, an' be *measur'bly* like I used to be, ez I am thet—Well, I'm that shore of it thet, though I don't to say favor divo'ces, I'd give you free leave to divo'ce me out of hand ef I don't. An' them fainty spells thet come over me sometimes, they ain't nothin' but heart weakness, the doctor says. But of co'se he don't know why it's weak—nor how it could be strengthened by the suppo't of yore love."

Mrs. Carroll felt no disposition to smile as she

glanced up into the speaker's thin, serious face. There was a new depth to his voice as he had thus confessed his life's secret—a depth that all his fervent confessions in public prayer had never revealed. It was still the prayer-meeting voice—*but more.*

Somehow, up to this time, while priding herself somewhat upon Billins's romantic attachment, she had never been able to take him quite seriously. It is hard to take a confirmed old bachelor seriously, his whole life seeming to give the lie to any fixed matrimonial intention. It is only when one knows the story, the personal *why* of the individual case, that she is able to admit her old-bachelor lover into the category of earnest suitors.

Indeed, it is doubtful whether or not one of these presumably self-elected celibates ever does make his tardy way with the desired woman without prefacing his suit with a touching explanation of "how it happened." That these explanations are usually lies does not alter the case.

But Billins was not lying, and Mrs. Carroll knew it as she looked at him. He was a thin, homely old man, absurd, perhaps, in his present rôle of aspirant to step-fatherhood, certainly so in his confident promise to return to youthful good looks, but for the first time in her life Mrs. Carroll saw him without a trace of the ridiculous. Indeed, so was her heart suddenly suffused with sympathy for the lonely man as he sat, a pathetic embodiment of self-abnegation before her, that, in the old-time confusion of tender sentiments, she felt for the moment that love had come into her life again—and she was startled.

Her next thoughts, by a strange and subtle connection, were of Eben Bradfield's children, and their motherless state — their ill-fitting clothes, their croupy tendencies.

What this had to do with anything David Billins or any other man chose to say to her, when she had many times wrathfully declared that she wouldn't marry that skinflint Eben Bradfield to save his life, she did not stop to ask herself. She simply realized a traitorous relation to the legacy of responsibility left at her door by her old-time neighbor and friend.

If she should marry another, Bradfield would *no doubt* forthwith start out and find him a bride: "an' like ez not she'd be some young chit of a girl thet wouldn't know no more about sewin' an' doin' for five child'en 'n nothin'."

These thoughts rushed through her mind with the rapidity of an electric current as she sat alone with Billins, listening to his story.

And just here it was that the sound of a croupy cough came to her from the front yard. Little Mary Bradfield was taking cold. It was time for the children to come in, and she did not hesitate a moment. What she said, however, was:

"You, Mamie Bradfield! *Oh,* Mamie!" And, when the little girl appeared before her, "Honey, I hear you a-coughin', an' it's time you was all *goin' in* now." She did not say "coming in"; she said, distinctly, "*going.*" "An' tell yore pa I say he better give you a spoonful o' that cough surrup I made you—*right away.*"

This speech, sending the entire crowd over to Bradfield's, was the first tangible encouragement Billins had received at her hands; and when Bradfield got her message, delivered in chorus by the crowd, he realized for the first time that Billins, as his rival, was to be taken in all seriousness. As to himself, he felt formally refused.

So elated was Billins over the little turn which it seemed to give his prospects that he took courage to draw his chair—it was the rustic one he had made for her—a little nearer the widow.

"Elder," she began, thoughtfully, before he had spoken again, "did John ever know about you wantin' to keep comp'ny with me?"

"John Carroll? No, ma'am, he didn't. Why, ef he'd 've knew it, I reckon you'd 've died a ol' maid, so far ez we two was concerned. We'd 'a' sat off an' twirled our thumbs, time out o' mind, neither one willin' to take advantage o' the other. No, ma'am, nobody atop o' this round world knew it but the good Lord an' the 'umble person thet's a-tellin' you now—*not another soul*, less 'n 'tis my guardeen angel. I did expec' thet that secret would 'a' been buried with me—in my coffin—an', tell the truth, Mis' Carroll, I've put down in my will thet I was to have a pink satin-lined one—not for myself, but because that secret was to lay in it.

"An' I'm a-talkin' right along—not stoppin' to see what you're a-fixin' to say. But ef you feel *shore* thet you couldn't never bring yourself to it—an' me so thin an' peaked, I wouldn't blame you much—but ef sech *is* the case, thet you couldn't consider it *no ways*, why, don't speak the word to-night. Let this be the one night in my life—even ef you're bound by conscience to write me a letter in the mornin'. I want to set here by yore side an' jest co't you for all I'm worth—for *this once-t*—an' ashamed of it am I not.

"I've took partic'lar pains, Mis' Carroll, ever sense the day I set out—which was the day follerin' yore full year o' widderhood—I've took partic'lar pains not to conceal nothin' from the Simpkinsville folks, an' they can't none of 'em point a finger at David Billins an' say he used to be a-spoonin' 'round with this girl an' that one—for spoons have I never traded in, not even in my sto'e. But I dare 'em *not* to say thet I have co'ted you *di*rec', straightforward an' outspoken, leavin' nothin' undone thet might, could, would, or should 'a' been done to prove myself yore devoted lover, world without end, Amen."

He paused here, and Mrs. Carroll felt almost as if she were in church, so familiar was his reverent voice in the oft-repeated form with which he closed his frequent prayers. She was really awed into silence. But Billins had soon resumed, his voice falling still lower.

"An' ef it all ends to-night, I reckon, by the help o' the good Lord, I can go back to my little house an' start fresh in the old track; but *nothin'* can't take *this* away, thet I've been permitted to set by yore side an' declare my heart. An' it 'll go down in Simpkinsville word-o'-mouth hist'ry thet David Billins loved an' co'ted Mary Carroll. It 'll be passed down in the *spoken* records that-a-way, even ef you don't 'low to have it recorded in the co't-house—which, with the blessin' o' the Lord an' the co't's seal, I trust it may be."

This sort of love-making was new to Mary Carroll. Never had man spoken to her after this manner before, and she was silenced in the presence of what seemed a more romantic and a loftier sentiment than she had known.

In the light of this new interpretation, all of Billins's conspicuous attentions took to themselves a fresh dignity. She, as well as the rest of Simpkinsville, had smiled when his mare appeared in the road, a bouquet of color illumined by the late sun, as he rode in with his floral offerings. She had smiled at his gallant speeches, laughed in her sleeve at the new expression of his figure as he met her with a courtly bow; but from this time forward, whatever the ultimate result of to-night's interview, she would be on his side. She would never be inclined to laugh again.

Indeed, the romantic avowal was very sweet to her woman's ears; but whether she was moved by the force of his passion, his fervor in its declaration, or was really falling seriously in love with the man, she did not for the moment know; but even while listening to the sound of his voice, she turned her eyes towards Bradfield's cottage and sighed. And then she said in all seriousness, and with a humility of manner that was an added charm:

"Elder, I'm very much afraid you've been deceived in me—all my life. You know, I never was, to say, very religious—an' I'm a mighty pore hand to go to communion, which you cert'n'y must know, ef you've taken notice. They's a heap o' better an' more religious women in Simpkinsville 'n what I am—an' for a man versed in Scripture verses an' gifted in prayer like you are—"

Billins raised his voice to speak, but she interrupted him.

"Don't say a word, Elder. I know myself, an' I know I'm awfully set on worldly vanities. Th' ain't a inch o' my house thet don't show it, too—not even to a pantry-shelf. The money I spend on colored paper for them shelves would buy a lot o' trac's for the conversion o' sinners, I know, an' the time I take notchin' it out in patterns I could be out distributin' 'em, too—an' yet I can't even say to you now that I'm resolved to do it. I ain't the trac'-distributin' sort. Even the religious habits I've been raised to don't seem to be very strong in me. Ef I'm purty tired of nights, 'stid of readin' a whole chapter o' Scripture, I don't hesitate to take a single verse. I did try to stick to readin' the full chapter, but I found myself a-readin' the hundred and seventeenth psalm purty near every night, till it was acchilly scand'lous, an' I got so ashamed of it thet I thought it 'd be mo' honest to take a verse or two outright somewheres else. So now that's what I most gen'rally do; an', tell the truth, some nights I don't disturb the Bible at all, but just say over to myself some verse I know, though I do try to say one thet 'll be a reproof to me for sech ungodliness. An' many a cold night have I said my prayers in bed. Don't say a word. I knew you'd be surprised, but I tell you some o' the church-goin' people you'd least suspect are the most wicked—an' I'm one of 'em. An' ez to worldly-mindedness *an'* vanity, why, I'm jest full of it. I do jest love a purty house."

"Of co'se you do, Mis' Carroll. An' why shouldn't you, I'd like to know? I like a purty house myself, though, to look at my little one room, nobody 'd think so. But I've had a sen-ti-ment about that little house o' mine—ever sence I put it up. Tell the truth, it ain't founded on nothin' *but* sen-ti-ment.

"You ricollec', I built that house befo' you was married. I wanted a place to sleep nights—outside o' the sto'e-house—an' so I built that right in the sto'e-house yard where it stands now; but I was determined then thet it mustn't be home-like or nice, for there was only one person in the world thet could ever make David Billins a home, an' that was Mary Sommers, which you then was. So I jest built that one room—good an' wide an' high—an' says I to myself, 'Ef the day ever comes when she gives her consents, why, then it 'll be for her to say where she wants rooms added on—always retainin' the one entrance-room for a middle hall.' That's why I finished off that front cornish so nice, an' put in that oak-grained door, with the little diamond winder-panes all round it.

"My house ain't no house, Mis' Carroll. It ain't a blessed thing but a front door an' hall to yore res-i-dence—whenever you're ready to take possession an' order the improvements. That's all it is, or ever has been. An' ez to yore bein' worldly-minded an' likin' purty things, why, that's a part of every wifely woman's life—to have an' keep things purty.

"An' when the Maker has set her sech a example ez He has set you, which you can't deny in the face of a merror, why—excuse me for chucklin' this-a-way, but all sech a woman ez you would have to do would be to try to live up to the beauty the Lord has laid on herself, an' to keep her surroundin's worthy o' that mark, which it 'd take a long purse an' a extravagant hand to do too, and keep half even."

Billins inclined his head in his characteristic old-school fashion as he closed this speech.

"I declare, Elder, you mustn't talk that-a-way." There was a note of real embarrassment in her protest.

"Yas, I must talk that-a-way, too, or else be dumb. Why, Mis' Carroll, you'd be jest ez out o' place in a bare, ugly house ez—well, ez I'd be, by my lonesome, awkward self, in a purty one—there!

"But remember they's jest ez beautiful a house a-waitin' for you out at my place ez you care to call for—an' plenty o' money for you to draw on whenever you care to let me set a rockin'-chair in the hall for you to rock in while you plan out the improvements.

"An' the trees are all set out so ez not to interfere with any reasonable plans you might have—an' they ain't one of 'em too good to chop down ef they're in yore way either. I set 'em that-a-way intentional. An' I thought maybe you'd like yore room on the south side, so I've set all the flowerin' trees that side—maginolias an' crape-myrtles an' camellias. An' that ol' catalpa-tree thet was there a'ready, I was a-fixin' to chop it out, an' seemed like it got wind of it an' started a-turnin' out special crops o' speckled-throated flowers to beg for its life. So

I left it there; but you might like it took out. It's a toler'ble coa'se tree—for yore side o' the house.

"Oh, how happy I am settin' here tellin' you all about it! Of co'se they was all set out befo' you was married; but I've always lived in that one room in the middle of a 'maginary house where you've came an' went through doors thet was never cut.

"Maybe some would say it wasn't right—an' you married to another—but I can't see the wrong of it, save my life, an' it has saved me many a lonely hour—that an', of co'se, the consolations o' faith.

"An' ez to yore claimin' not to be religious, why, I reckon I've done enough prayin' an' Bible-readin' for both of us. It nachilly takes mo' watchfulness an' prayer to keep a man straight than it does a woman, special when the Lord *created* her ez near perfec' ez He dared—without clair breakin' His rule for mortals on this mundane sp'ere."

"I *do* declare you *mustn't* talk that-a-way, Elder. It ain't right. I'm so far off from *half* perfect, even, thet I feel like a hypocrite jest a-listenin' at you. Here come them child'en o' mine 'crost the stile now, an' I'm ready to bet thet Mary Bradfield is sick, an' they've sent for me.

"Yes, I knew it soon ez I see you child'en comin' 'crost the stile"—she was now addressing the group, who by this time had announced their errand.

Mamie Bradfield was sick, but Eben had not sent for his neighbor. His message was simply that he had given the prescribed dose of croup syrup; the child continued hoarse; should he give another?

"And, mamma," the little Carroll girl added, "I think maybe you better come over, 'cause little Mamie is a-breathin' awful whistly."

Mrs. Carroll thought so too, and so did Billins, who forthwith rose, awkwardly wondering if he could do anything to help.

"Cert'n'y, Elder; you better come right along with me," she answered, quickly; and then she added—prudentially, "You know, she might get worse, an' you could go for the doctor."

And so, the children leading the way, they hurried across to Bradfield's house.

As she mounted the stile, standing thus in the very centre of his proposed hall to unite the two houses, the widow could not help instituting a comparison between this and Billins's actual hall awaiting her commands, a mile away.

To her mind this one was simply a practical economic scheme; the other expressed the devotion of a life. And yet her own life and its interests were rooted here. She sighed as she stepped lightly off the stoop on the Bradfield side.

But there was no time now for selfish thought. The "whistly breathing" of the little sufferer had by this time become a hoarse bark, and at the sound of it Mrs. Carroll quickened her steps; then, turning hurriedly, she sent Billins in haste for the doctor. But, shame to tell, when his slim figure disappeared among the trees, the thought that took shape in her mind, as she followed the children in, was precisely this:

"I'd like to know what good it did Susan Bradfield to die, anyhow. She'd ought to 've stayed right here an' looked after her child'en—that's what she'd ought to 've done!"

But when she had entered, her voice was very womanly and tender as she held out her arms and said:

"Lemme hold 'er, Eben."

She had called Bradfield by his first name only at rare intervals during his life—in times of affliction—and her doing so now was a first danger-signal to the father's slow ears. It alarmed him more than had the metallic cough or the ever-turning head of the restless child struggling for breath in his arms.

But the warning note had come in a voice of sympathy, and his heart went out of him afresh to both child and woman as he laid the little one in her arms. And his being was flooded with a great wave of pain in the presence of the imminent loss of both. Then came the boon of loving service—tending the one, obeying the other.

Mrs. Carroll, gentle, alert, maternal, was entire mistress of the situation, while poor Bradfield, not having the sick-nurse faculty—a rare endowment, indeed, to his sex—blundered like an awkward boy as he mutely did her bidding, his only words being disconnected terms of endearment spoken to the sick child.

The first half-hour spent thus was one of those pocket editions of eternity that mortals are sometimes bidden to read at a sitting, and it would be hard to say whether to man, woman, or child it seemed longest—to which it was fraught with keenest pain.

There was at least nothing complex in the child's simple physical battle for breath.

By what mental or emotional process the neighbor-woman came into vital concern in the matter does not at present appear, nor, indeed, looking in upon her as she calmly took charge of things, changing chaos to order by a few masterful strokes, would one suspect that the heart guiding the executive hand was in the first tremors of a conviction involving heavy issues and painful complexities. And, too, her mother-heart was deeply touched for the frail little one whose mother-needing life hung so lightly in the balance before her. But dominating all was the woman of faculty—the woman who knew equally well how to get the sleepy children noiselessly to bed without exciting a suspicion of danger, and to secure the needed services of the half-asleep old darky nodding in the doorway by the exactly reverse policy of scaring her into wakefulness—a bit of tact exemplified in a nutshell in the following sentence spoken in the old negro's ear while Bradfield's back was turned:

"Aunt Randy, step around quietly an' get them child'en off to bed, where they belong, an' don't let 'em know how bad off Mamie is. Then, ef you'll get some water het right quick, an' some mustard mixed 'g'inst the doctor's orders, maybe we can bring her through—ef she don't choke to death 'fo' the doctor gets here. An' drive that black cat away, for gracious' sakes, 'fo' she *meaows* in the doorway. We don't want any death-signs to-night!"

Nothing was forgotten in the pressure of the moment—not even the setting of a lantern in the front door, so that the doctor should see his way clearly up the walk.

This thoughtful provision was not destined to serve its purpose to-night, however. The little patient passed the crisis of her disease, and fell into a feverish sleep in Mrs. Carroll's lap without professional treatment. And the lantern burned all night in the doorway.

When the necessity for the doctor was passed, and the prospect of his visit reduced to a minimum by the coming of the "wee short hours," Mrs. Carroll forbore to remove the light, which was as a third personality, sharing the watch with her and Bradfield, its bright eye exercising over the two a sort of friendly chaperonage—a word entirely foreign to her vocabulary.

Bradfield, poor in speech even when presenting a definite plea, was wellnigh dumb to-night. He sat at a distance from her, and when the danger was passed he drew his chair quite to the opposite side of the room, whence from time to time he timidly ventured such expressions of commonplace solicitude as the following: "I'm 'fear'd you'll be completely wo'e out settin' up all night this-a-way, Mis' Carroll."

Mrs. Carroll was not worn out physically, but her patience was wellnigh threadbare, and her state of mind towards Billins such as to fill her soul with criminations of self. She had *known*, as soon as she had come into the presence of the silent man in his extremity, that Billins's case was utterly hopeless. The revulsion of feeling was as absolute as it was sudden, and she resented it in herself as fiercely as she had hitherto resented Bradfield's parsimony, as indeed she resented it yet.

This was why the first hour of her watch with him was one of torture. She felt the restfulness of his quiet presence, and she resented even that.

Billins had courted her in prodigal fashion, sparing nothing, even to his own dignity. His words were buzzing in her ears yet, but they were as a swarm of bees that worried and wearied her. The perfume of romance with which they had fallen from his fluent lips was supplanted in the brief retrospect by the all-pervading odors of shaving-soap and orris root. So other personal touches that had eluded her at the moment presented themselves in the after-view. The fascination had been a thing of an hour, and the hour was past.

She would have to write him a letter in the morning, and she would almost rather die than do it; for, treat it as she might, she could not doubt the sincerity of his declaration.

It was nearly day when finally she slipped the sleeping child gently into her cradle and rose to go. Bradfield had risen with her, and stood on the other side of the cradle.

She afterwards said, in recalling this moment, that she was as much surprised and frightened as he professed to have been at the sound of her own voice, as she said, looking up into his face:

"Eben, set down there a minute; I want to talk to you." Indeed, she roundly denied afterwards that she had spoken these words, to which Bradfield laughingly agreed that she had not, "but the Lord had spoken 'em through her." And perhaps he was right, for when he had seated himself on his side of the cradle she said, slowly: "Eben, the Lord knows what I'm goin' to say to you, for I don't. But there's one thing shore. You can't live along this way any longer. I won't allow it. I've got to have these child'en where I can do for 'em right.

"But I ain't quite ez mean-sperited ez you think I am, either. There ain't a man livin' atop o' this earth thet I'd allow to marry me for an economy—not even you. Ef I'm married, I've got to be married ez an *extravagance worth bein' afforded*, an' that's all there is to it.

"Don't say a word, now. I've been burstin' for a year, an' when it's all out I'll feel better.

An' I'll tell you what I've got to say: Ef you'll promise me to have that dividin'-fence chopped up for firewood, or made into a bonfire nex' Democrat you help 'lect for Congress, I'll say to take it down; but I don't want picket or post of it ever set up on my premises, long ez I live. An' ef you ca'culate to set a middle hall in here, throwin' the two houses into one, which 'll be the handiest thing *to* do, why, I don't want any money saved on it—I'd ruther see it wasted; an' that's all I've got to say. An' you can think it over, an' set me against the expense, an' balance the accounts, an' let me know.

"An' nex' time she stirs give 'er fo' drops out o' this bottle, an' I reckon she better have her little shoes an' stockin's on in the mornin' till the day warms up."

She had risen and was moving towards the door, but Bradfield caught her, and had thrown his long arms clear around her shoulders before she could resist. Thus, with eyes swimming in tears, he confronted her.

"My God! Mary Carroll!" This was all he could say, but he held her tight until he should recover his voice. And just then it was that the lantern keeping guard at the door tumbled over and went suddenly out. There are times when the chaperon does well to close her eyes.

The rolling over of the lantern of its own accord was an improbable phenomenon, and when Bradfield and Mrs. Carroll started to investigate it, they walked discreetly, arm's-length apart, to meet the doctor's dog ambling across the porch.

The doctor was "just passing," and, seeing the light, dropped in to ascertain its cause—and, he might have added, to tell the news. He had been out all night—was just getting home.

"A sad night of it, Bradfield—a sad night, Mis' Carroll," he said, looking hard at her as he stood in the door. "I never closed a better man's eyes in my life 'n I've jest now closed. Elder Billins has gone to join the congregation on the other side. Come to my office early in the evenin', an' seemed to be tryin' to talk an' couldn't—had one o' them heart-failin' spells—so I give him some drops, an' he come to a little, an' I drove him home, an' set there with 'im a hour or so, talkin' along, an' he listenin' but not sayin' a word, an' treckly he went off again same way—not a rack o' pain, smilin' in the face—an' I brought 'im through again, an' he bettered up, so he started to talk, but his words, straight enough some ways, was all wrong others. Didn't seem to know rightly where he was; 'lowed he was in yore front hall, Mis' Carroll, an' he stuck to it. An' so, seein' he was bad off, I drove out an' fetched in a couple o' the neighbors to set with him. But, time we got there, he had reached the gates an' was enterin' in."

Mrs. Carroll's face was rigid and white as she listened. Neither she nor Bradfield spoke for some time; but finally he said, slowly:

"He *was* in her hall to-night, doctor, settin' an' talkin'—an' like ez not, he thought he was there yet. He went for you for my little Mamie. She's had the worst attackt o' croup she's ever had; but Mis' Carroll has nursed her through it. But I reckon this night 'll be one we'll both remember all our days." He looked at her as he spoke. And then he added, with real feeling: "Pore Billins! I can't rightly seem to realize it. Ez good a man ez ever walked the earth."

"Yes," replied the doctor. "I've known the ins an' outs o' Billins's life for twenty year, off an' on, an' I tell you he was one in a thousand."

"Yas, he was," said Mrs. Carroll.

MISS JEMIMA'S VALENTINE

MISS JEMIMA'S VALENTINE

TWO crimson spots appeared upon Miss Jemima's pale face when she heard the gate-latch click. She knew that her brother was bringing in the mail, and, as he entered the room, she bent lower over her work, her crochet-needle flew faster, and she coughed a slight, nervous cough. But she did not look up.

She saw without looking that her brother held a pile of valentines in his hand, and she knew that when presently he should have finished distributing them to his eager sons and daughters, her nephews and nieces, he would come and bring one to her—or else? he would not do this last. It was this uncertainty that deepened the crimson spots upon her cheeks.

If there was one for her he would presently come, and, leaning over her shoulder, he would say, as he dropped upon her lap the largest, handsomest of them all, "This looks mighty suspicious, Sis' 'Mimie," or, "We'll have to find out about this," or maybe, as he presented it, he would covertly shield her by addressing himself to the younger crowd after this fashion:

"Ef I was a lot o' boys an' girls, an' couldn't git a bigger valentine from all my sweethearts an' beaux than my ol' auntie can set still at home an' git, why, I'd quit tryin'—that's what I would."

There was always a tenderness in the brother's manner when he handed his sister her valentine. He had brought her one each year for seven years now, and after the first time, when he had seen the look of pain and confusion that had followed his playful teasing, he had never more than relieved the moment by a passing jest.

The regular coming of "Aunt Jemima's valentine" was a mystery in the household.

It had been thirteen years since she had quarrelled with Eli Taylor, her lover, and they had parted in anger, never to meet again. Since then she had stayed at home and quietly grown old.

Fourteen years ago she had been in the flush of this her only romance, and St. Valentine's Day had brought a great, thick envelope, in which lay, fragrant with perfume, a gorgeous valentine. Upon this was painted, after an old Dresden-china pattern, a beautiful lady with slender waist and corkscrew curls, standing beside a tall cavalier, who doffed his hat to her as he presented the envelope that bore her name, so finely and beautifully written that only very young eyes could read it unaided.

By carefully opening this tiny envelope one might read the printed rhyme within—the rhyme so tender and loving that it needed only the inscription of a name on the flap above it to make it all-sufficient in personal application to even the most fastidious.

This gorgeous valentine was so artfully constructed that, by drawing its pictured front forward, it could be made to stand alone, when there appeared a fountain in the background and a brilliant peacock with argus-eyed tail, a great rose on a tiny bush, and a crescent moon. The older children had been very small when this resplendent confection had come into their home. Some of them were not born, but they had all grown up in the knowledge of it.

There had been times in the tender memories of all of them when "Aunt 'Mimie" had taken them into her room, locked the door, and, because they had been very good, let them take a peep at her beautiful valentine, which she kept carefully hidden away in her locked bureau drawer.

They had even on occasions been allowed to wash their hands and hold it—just a minute.

It had always been a thing to wonder over, and once—but this was the year it came, when her sky seemed as rosy as the ribbon she wore about her waist—Miss Jemima had stood it up on the whatnot in the parlor when the church sociable met at her brother's house, and everybody in town had seen it, while for her it made the whole room beautiful.

But the quarrel had soon followed—Eli had gone away in anger—and that had been the end.

Disputes over trifles are the hardest to mend, each party finding it hard to forgive the other for being angry for so slight a cause.

And so the years had passed.

For six long years the beautiful valentine had lain carefully put away. For five years Jemima had looked at it with tearless eyes and a hardened heart. And then came the memorable first anniversary when the children of the household began to celebrate the day, and tiny, comic-pictured pages began flitting in from their school sweethearts. The realization of the new era was a shock to Miss Jemima. In the youthful merriment of those budding romances she seemed to see a sort of reflection of her own long-ago joy, and in the faint glow of it she felt impelled to go to her own room and to lock the door and look at the old valentine.

With a new, strange tremor about her heart and an unsteady hand she took it out, and when in the light of awakened emotion she saw once more its time-stained face and caught its musty odor, she seemed to realize again the very body of her lost love, and for the first time in all the years the fountains of her sorrow were broken up, and she sobbed her tired heart out over the old valentine.

Is there a dead-hearted woman in all God's beautiful world, I wonder, who would not weep again, if she could, over life's yellowing symbols —symbols of love gone by, of passion cooled— who would not feel almost as if in the recovery of her tears she had found joy again?

If Miss Jemima had not found joy, she had at least found her heart once more—and sorrow. Her life had been for so long a dreary, treeless plain that, in the dark depth of the valley of sorrowing, she realized, as sometimes only from sorrow's deeps poor mortals may know it, the possible height of bliss.

For the first time since the separation, she clasped the valentine to her bosom and called her lover's name over and over again, sobbing it, without hope, as one in the death-agony. But such emotion is not of death. Is it not, rather, a rebirth—a rebirth of feeling? So it was with Miss Jemima, and the heart-stillness that had been her safety during all these years would not return to her again. There would never more be a time when her precious possession would not have a sweet and vital meaning to her—when it would not be a tangible embodiment of the holiest thing her life had known.

From this time forward, stirred by the budding romances about her, Miss Jemima would repair for refuge and a meagre comfort to that which, while in its discolored and fading face it denied none of life's younger romance, still gave her back her own.

The woman of forty may never realize her years in the presence of her contemporaries. Forty women of forty might easily feel young enough to scoff at the bald head, and deserve to be eaten by bears—but thirty-nine with a budding-maid-for-fortieth scoffer? Never!

Miss Jemima, in her suddenly realized young-love setting, had become, to her own consciousness, old and of a date gone by. "Aunt Jemima" was naturally regarded by her blooming nephews and nieces, as well as by their intimates, who wore their incipient mustaches still within their conscious top lips, or dimples dancing in their ruddy cheeks, quite in the same category as Mrs. Gibbs who was sixty, or any of their aunts and grandmothers who sat serenely in daguerreotype along the parlor mantel.

But there is apt to come a time in the life of the live single woman of forty—if she be alive enough—when, in the face of even negative and affectionate disparagement, she is moved to declare herself.

Perhaps there may be some who would say that this declaration savors of earth. Even so, the earth is the Lord's. It is one thing to be a flower pasted in a book and quite another to be the bud a maiden wears—one thing to be To-day, and another to be Yesterday.

One thing, indeed, it was to own a yellow, time-stained valentine, and quite a different one to be of the dimpled throng who crowded the Simpkinsville post-office on Valentine's Day.

"I reckon them young ones would think it was perfec'ly re-dic'lous ef I was to git a valentine at my time o' life," Miss Jemima said, aloud, to her looking-glass one morning. It was the day before St. Valentine's, of the year following that which held her day of tears.

"*But I'll show 'em,*" she added, with some resolution, as she turned to her bureau drawer.

And she did show them. On the next day a great envelope addressed to Miss Jemima Martha Sprague came in with the package of lesser favors, and Miss Jemima suddenly found herself the absorbing centre of a new interest—an interest that, after having revolved about her a while, flew off in suspicion towards every superannuated bachelor or widower within a radius of thirty miles of Simpkinsville.

It had been a great moment for Miss Jemima when the valentine came in, and a trying one when, with genuine old-time blushes, she had been constrained to refuse to open it for the crowd.

How she felt an hour later when, in the secrecy of her own chamber, she took from its new envelope her own old self-sent valentine, only He who has tender knowledge of maidenly reserves and sorrows will ever know.

There was something in her face when she reappeared in the family circle that forbade a cruel pursuit of the theme, and so, after a little playful bantering, the subject was dropped.

But the incident had lifted her from one condition into quite another in the family regard, and Miss Jemima found herself unconsciously living up to younger standards.

But this was seven years ago, and the mysterious valentine had become a yearly fact.

There had never been any explanations. When pressed to the wall Miss Jemima had, indeed, been constrained to confess that "cert'n'y—why of co'se every valentine she had ever got had been sent her by a man." (How sweet and sad this truth !)

"And are all the new ones as pretty as your lovely old one, Aunt 'Mimie ?"

To this last query she had carefully replied :

"I 'ain't never got none thet ain't every bit an' grain ez purty ez that one—not a one."

"An' why don't you show 'em to us, then ?"

Such obduracy was indeed hard to comprehend.

If, as the years passed, her brother began to suspect, he made no sign of it, save in an added tenderness. And, of course, he could not know.

On the anniversary upon which this little record of her life has opened, the situation was somewhat exceptional.

The valentine had hitherto always been mailed in Simpkinsville—her own town. This post-mark had been noted and commented upon, and yet it had seemed impossible to have it otherwise. But this year, in spite of many complications and difficulties, she had resolved that the envelope should tell a new story.

The farthest point from which, within her possible acquaintance, it would naturally hail was the railroad town of—let us call it Hope.

The extreme difficulty in the case lay in the fact that the post-office here was kept by her old lover, Eli Taylor.

Here for ten years he had lived his reticent bachelor days, selling ploughs and garden seed and cotton prints and patent medicines, and keeping post-office in a small corner of his store.

Everybody knows how a spot gazed at intently for a long time changes color—from green to red and then to white.

As Miss Jemima pondered upon the thought of sending herself a valentine through her old lover's hands, the color of the scheme began to change from impossible green to rosy red.

The point of objection became, in the mysterious evolution, its objective point.

Instead of dreading, she began ardently to desire this thing.

By the only possible plan through which she could manage secretly to have the valentine mailed in Hope—a plan over which she had lost sleep, and in which she had been finally aided by an illiterate colored servant—it must reach her on the day before Valentine's. This day had come and gone, and her treasure had not returned to her. Had the negro failed to mail it? Had it remained all night in the post-office—in possession of her lover? Would she ever see it again?

* * * * * * *

Would her brother ever, *ever*, EVER get through his trifling with the children and finish distributing their valentines?

* * * * * * *

It was not very long to wait—a minute, perhaps half a minute—and yet it seemed an age before the distribution was over, and she felt rather than saw her brother moving in her direction.

"Bigger an' purtier one 'n ever for Aunt 'Mimie this time—looks to me like," he said, as at last he laid the great envelope upon her trembling knee.

"Don't reckon it's anything extry—in partic'-lar," she answered, not at all knowing what she said, as she continued her work, leaving the valentine where he had dropped it; not touching it, indeed, until she presently wound up her yarn in answer to the supper-bell. Then she took it, with her work-basket, into her own room, and, dropping it into her upper bureau drawer, turned the key.

The moment when she broke the seal each

year—late at night, alone in her locked chamber—had always been a sad one to Miss Jemima, and to-night it was even sadder than ever. She had never before known how she cared for this old love-token.

As she sat to-night looking at the outside of the envelope, turning it over and over in her thin hands, great hot tears fell upon it and ran down upon her fingers; but she did not heed them. It was, indeed, a meagre little embodiment of the romance of a life; but, such as it was, she would not part with it. She would never send it out from her again—never, never, never.

It was even dearer now than ever before, after this recent passage through her lover's hands. She raised it lovingly and laid it against her cheek. Could he have handled it and passed it on without a thought of her? Impossible. And since he had thought of her, what must have been the nature of his thoughts? Was he jealous—jealous because somebody was sending his old sweetheart a valentine?

This year's envelope, selected with great pains and trouble from a sample catalogue and ordered from a distant city, was a fine affair, profusely decorated with love symbols.

For a long time Miss Jemima sat enjoying a

strange sense of nearness to her lover, before she felt inclined to confront the far-away romance typified by the yellowed sheet within. And yet she wanted to see even this again—to realize it.

And so, with thoughts both eager and fearful, she finally inserted a hair-pin carefully in the envelope, ripping it open delicately on two sides, so that the valentine might come out without injury to its frail, perforated edges. Then, carefully holding its sides apart, she shook it.

And now—?

One of God's best traits is that He doesn't tell all He knows—and sees.

How Miss Jemima felt or acted—whether she screamed or fainted—no one will ever know, when, instead of the familiar pictured thing, there fell into her lap a beautiful brand-new valentine.

It was certainly a long time before she recovered herself enough to take the strange thing into her hands, and when she did so it was with fingers that trembled so violently that a bit of paper that came within it fluttered and fell beyond her reach. There it lay for fully several minutes before she had strength to move from her seat to recover it.

There was writing on the fluttering fragment, but what it was, and why Miss Jemima wept over it and read it again and again, are other trifling things that perhaps God does well not to tell.

The details of other people's romances are not always interesting to outsiders.

However, for a better understanding of this particular case it may be well to know that the servant who took charge of the old lover's room in Hope, and who had an investigating way with her, produced seven or eight torn scraps of paper collected at this period from his scrap-basket, on which were written bits of broken sentences like the following: "—sending you this new valentine just as hearty as I sent the old one fourteen years—"

"You sha'n't never want for a fresh one again every year long as I live, unless you take—"

"—if you want the old one back again, unless you take me along with it."

It is generally conceded that one of the lowest things that even a very depraved and unprincipled person ever does is to intercept and read other people's letters. To print them or otherwise make them public is a thing really too contemptible to contemplate in ordinary circumstances. But this case, if intelligently considered, seems somewhat exceptional, for, be it borne in mind, all these writings, without exception, and a few others too sacred to produce even here, are the things that Eli Taylor, postmaster, *did not* send to his old sweetheart, Jemima Martha Sprague.

Miss Jemima always burned her scraps, and so, even had it seemed well to condescend to seek similar negative testimony concerning her laboriously written reply, it would have been quite impossible to find any. Certain it is, however, that she posted a note on the following day, and that a good many interesting things happened in quick succession after this.

And then—

There was a little, quiet, middle-aged wedding in the church on Easter Sunday. It was the old lover's idea to have it then, as he said their happiness was a resurrection from the dead, and it was befitting to celebrate it at the blessed Easter season.

Miss Jemima showed her new valentine to the family before the wedding came off, but, in spite of all their coaxing and begging, she observed a rigid reticence in regard to all those that had come between that and the old one. And so, seeing the last one actually in evidence, and rejoicing in her happiness, they only smiled and whispered that they supposed he and she had been "quar'lin' it out on them valentines, year by year, and on'y now got to the place where they could make up."

The old man, Eli, in spite of his indomitable pride, had come out of his long silence with all due modesty, blaming himself for many things.

"I ain't fitten for you, Jemimy, honey, no mo'n I was fo'teen year ago," he said, while his arm timidly sought her shoulder the night before the wedding, "but ef you keered enough about me to warm over the one little valentine I sent you nigh on to fifteen year ago, and to make out to live on it, I reckon I can keep you supplied with jest ez good diet ez that—fresh every day an' hour. But befo' I take you into church I want to call yo' attention to the fac' thet I'm a criminal befo' the law, li'ble to the state's-prison for openin' yo' mail—an' ef you say so, why, I'll haf to go."

"Well, Eli," Miss Jemima answered, quite seriously, "ef you're li'ble to state's-prison for what you done, I don't know but I'm worthy to go to a hotter place—for the deceit I've practised. Ef actions speak louder than words, I've cert'n'y been guilty of an annual lie which I've in a manner swo'e to every day I've lived up to it. Still, I observed all the honesty I could. Nights the old valentine would be out, I never could sleep good, an' they was times when I was tempted to put blank sheets in the envelope, an' ef I had 'a' done it I don't know whether the truth would 'a' prevailed under the children's quizzin' or not. Children are mighty gifted in puttin' leadin' questions. We are weak creatures, Eli, an' prone to sin. Yas, takin' it all 'round, I reckon I'm a worse criminal 'n you—an' ef I got my dues, I'd be—"

"Well," said Eli, "I reckon, ef the truth was told, the place where we jest nachelly both b'long is the insane asylum—for the ejiots we've acted. When I reflect thet I might 'a' been ez happy ez I am now fo'teen year ago, an' think about all the time we've lost— Of co'se, honey, I know I had no earthly right to open yo' valentine, an' yet—"

"Where'd we be now, ef you hadn't 've opened it, Eli?"

"—or ef you hadn't 've *sent* it to me, honey, directed to yo' dear self, with a J for Jemimy different from anybody else's J's on earth."

"Why, Eli! You don't mean—"

"Yas, I do, too. I knowed that flag-topped J of yores, jest ez soon ez—"

"But, Eli, I feel awful!"

"You needn't, dearie. *I* don't."

And he kissed her—square on the lips.

"An' I don't now, neither."

And he did it again.

A SLENDER ROMANCE

A SLENDER ROMANCE

DEACON HATFIELD was forty-five years old and a bachelor. And he was a good bachelor. Now, a good bachelor is an object to sigh over so long as there is a worthy unmarried maid available.

At least, such is the feeling in Simpkinsville. And so the best Simpkinsville folk, who unanimously regarded the deacon as one good husband gone wrong, sighed as they passed from contemplation of his wasted domestic qualities to the solitary life of a certain Miss Euphemia Twiggs, commonly known as "Miss Phemie," who, during her nearly forty years of residence among them, had proved by many signs her entire fitness for the position of wife to the deacon. The deacon was mild and gentle of mien. Miss Phemie was a woman of decision. She would have given him just the accent he seemed to require for his full perfection.

And then she needed—if such things are ever needs—a home-setting and personal endorsement. It is one thing to be endorsed by a community, and quite another to have the individual endorsement and protection of a special and particular man. The woman thus equipped presents her credentials every time she gives her name. For Mrs. John Smith and all that relates to her, see John Smith, Esquire. Now John Smith's name may not have great value among men; but his wife, simply because she may appropriate it, has a certain social prestige not quite attainable by the unmarried woman, even though she be far her superior.

At least, so it is in Simpkinsville. So are social values in some of the world's secluded spots still reckoned upside down.

For many years the good people of the good little village had regarded Miss Phemie and the deacon as definitely in need of each other. It would never have been granted for a moment that either could need any one else. The deacon had seen the young women of the community grow up, blossom into beauty, and marry, one by one, and he had stood aside and let them depart.

Miss Euphemia had likewise seen men come and go. It is true, however, that she had been several times "kep' company with" in years past, and once, at least, unequivocally addressed by a worthy man, now the father of one of Simpkinsville's leading families. This of course gave her a certain reserve of dignity, to be drawn upon on occasion, that was in itself a distinction.

Nevertheless, she remained "Euphemia O. Twiggs" on both church-books and tax-roll; for, be it understood, Miss Twiggs was no pauper.

Her income of four or five hundred dollars a year, varying with the crops, gave her a financial independence that went far to dignify her position. And yet, so playfully is the single life regarded in some localities, and so delicate was Miss Euphemia's poise between the independent single woman she consciously was and the possible heroine of an always imminent romance, that the village folk never lost an opportunity of tipping the balance for their own amusement. Thus when, at one of the church sociables, she was prevailed upon to sing Tennyson's "Song of the Brook," a favorite number in the village repertoire, on her rendering of the words,

> "For men may come and men may go,
> But I go on forever,"

there was a suppressed titter among the young and giddy set in the back of the assembly, and one or two of the more adventurous craned their necks to look at the deacon, who was observed to clear his throat. But this may have been accidental. Certainly Miss Euphemia was wholly unaware of any personal application of her song to herself.

But another thing was equally sure: the deacon and she were distinctly aware of each other. Indeed, it would have been tacitly conceded by every one that for either to marry a third person would have been an act approaching discourtesy to the one remaining.

Still, be it said to their credit, both had been frequently known separately to declare their unchangeable intentions of remaining forever single. But this was always under pressure of the village bantering; and what is the value of such protestation from man or woman pressed to the wall?

There had possibly been moments of annoyance in the lives of each of these good people when the marriage of either to a third person would have been a definite relief to the other. As one of Miss Euphemia's friends had said to her on one occasion:

"Th' ain't no fun in havin' your whole livelong life overshaddered by a man with no earthly intentions."

To which way of stating the case Miss Euphemia had replied with some spirit:

"Which ef he had any intentions, he'd be welcome to keep 'em to hisself."

But, again, what woman could have been expected to say less under the circumstances?

There had been other old bachelors and maidens in and about Simpkinsville. Indeed, several were there now, but to all excepting these two were attached their individual romances, long ago finished in tragedy, or still pending.

There was actually, as she herself asserted, "nothing" between Miss Euphemia and the deacon, not even a professed personal friendship. The point was that there *ought to be.* He had never paid her a visit in his life. He had simply for twenty-five years, more or less, sat in the pew behind her at church, found the hymns as they were given out, and then, leaning forward, changed hymn-books with her.

That was all.

This was only the part of good manners, according to the Simpkinsville code polite, and he would have done the same for any other woman sitting unattended in the pew before him.

For her to decline his book would have been embarrassing at first, and, as the years passed, it would have been serious to do so. Indeed, it would easily have been construed into refusing a man before he had offered himself. And not entirely without cause, either, as an ulterior motive would have been immediately apparent, and there was absolutely nothing back of the small courtesy but himself—himself, eligible, not asking for her.

So Miss Euphemia continued to sing from the deacon's book, and the years went on. A little thin spot was beginning to show on the back of the deacon's head, and a tiny hollow, corresponding with the one at the base of her throat, was coming in between the cords at the back of Miss Euphemia's neck. It was as if Time, in passing down the aisle, had laid his palm lightly upon the man's pate, and then, in a spirit of mischievous spite, had jabbed the back of the woman's sensitive neck with his peaked thumb.

Some of Time's revenges are so shabby that we find it hard to forgive them in one so old—one who ought, centuries ago, to have learned to be kindly at least.

The deacon saw the old man's finger-mark upon the slender neck before him, but Miss Euphemia, seated in front of him, did not see the threatening baldness of his head. Still, of course, she knew it was there. Everybody in Simpkinsville knew just how bald, or nearly bald,

W. MC NAIR JR.

or how far from it, everybody else was. They even knew who secretly pulled out gray hairs, and how old some people were who would never be bald or gray, because it didn't run in their families to be so, and their luxuriant locks were held at a corresponding discount or premium according to the point of observation.

There was no reason up to this point in their lives to believe that either Miss Euphemia or the deacon was especially interested in the fact that the other was growing old, or, indeed, that they were particularly interested in each other at all. If they had been let alone, it seems quite probable that they would have continued to the end of their lives to sing from each other's books in their adjoining pews, and this one point of neighborly contact in their separate lives might never have been made a pivotal one, as it was destined to become through the playful intermeddling of interested friends.

It was the minister who began it. At a little supper spread for the officers of the church at the house of one of the elders, he was the most frivolous guest present. The popular after-dinner "curse-word story" of the cloth would never have been tolerated in Simpkinsville, even with its naughty periods reduced to whispers. And so the dominie's mischievous spirit found vent in missiles of inordinate teasing. After spending his lighter fire in several directions, he said, finally, with an assumption of great seriousness, addressing his opposite neighbor, the schoolmaster of the village, and turning his back upon the deacon as he spoke :

"I've been tryin' to make a mathematical calculation, Brother Clark, and I think I'll have to get you to come in with your arithmetic and help me out. I'd like to estimate exactly how many times in twenty-three years Deacon Hatfield and Miss Euphemia Twiggs have changed hymn-books."

Of course there was boisterous laughter at this proposition ; but the Rev. Mr. Bowen, who spoke as one with authority, quickly restored silence with a wave of his hand.

"No, I'm not a-jokin'," he continued ; "I've been a-puzzlin' over this calculation for some time. Twenty-three years of 52 Sundays makes 1196. But, you see, there's—

"Wait ; le' me get out my pencil an' paper again. I thought I had them figgurs all worked out in my mind, but they're a little too many for me.

"Here it is. Now, I'll call 'em out as I put 'em down : Once every Sunday for 23 years would be 1196 times ; but, you see, there's three hymns sung every Sunday mornin', an' two every Sun-

"'I'D LIKE TO ESTIMATE EXACTLY HOW MANY TIMES'"

day evenin', an' three at prayer-meetin'. That makes eight book-swappin's for every week for *singin'*; an' countin' in the useless handin' back o' the book at every mornin' service—what I'd designate as a empty swap—why, that makes nine a week. Now, nine times 1196 comes to 10,764, which, added to special meetin's that's been held throughout the year, an' such little extries as the singin' of doxologies—exceptin', of co'se, the long metre, which they do manage to worry through without changin' books; an' I confess to you now that I have sometimes given out doxologies of other metres just to see 'em swap books, they *do* do it so purty—" He paused here in deliberate invitation of the laughter that followed. "I say, allowin' for all such extries, an' what time there may be over and above twenty-three years, which there is, more or less, with sech odds an' ends as an occasional leap-year Sunday thrown in, if my arithmetic is anyway right—why, they're consid'ble past the 12,000 notch, *easy*.

"Now, the next question is—an' maybe this is mo' a question in algebra than it is of arithmetic, 'cause there's a unknown quantity somewhere in it—the next question is, how many of such open attentions as this—which we all know to be entirely unnecessary, as both parties can read both words and numbers at sight—how many of such attentions, I say, does it take to be equivalent to an open an' above-boa'd proposal of marriage?

"It seems to me that it wouldn't be any more than fair to require that after ten or twelve thousand times there ought to be an understandin' either to have 'em *mean* somethin' or *quit*—one!

"Now, what do you say? I put it to vote, an' if there is a tie, why, I say, give Brother Hatfield the castin' vote. Otherwise, let him maintain the same discreet silence he's been maintainin' these twenty-three years an' over."

He paused here as if to take breath, whereupon the entire party, convulsed with laughter throughout, burst into most uproarious applause; all excepting the deacon, whose usually pale face resembled nothing so much as a fibrous and gnarled little beet lifted from the soaked earth after a shower, as he sat grinning helplessly in the midst of his tormentors. For of course all were with the minister in anything he might dare in behalf of their long-desired match.

Seeing his advantage, he was soon pursuing it again:

"But, my brethren, before the votin' commences," he interrupted, securing silence now by assuming for the moment his ministerial voice—"before the votin' begins, I say, I'd like to call attention to one or two other points in this case. I have ascertained by exact measurement with a spirit-level—which I felt free to do, bein' your spiritual adviser—I have ascertained that the top edge of the back of Miss Euphemia's pew is worn down a little over an inch in exac'ly the spot where those twelve thousand passin's of hymn-books have taken place. Now, takin' that fig-ur'tively and as a basis of mathematical calcu-lations at once, it seems to me that we could safely say that in time this romance, if left to its own co'se, would finally wear away all barriers 'twixt the two pews. *In time,* I say, but *how much time?* That's the mathematical question.

"Even grantin' that Miss Euphemia an' Brother Hatfield have found the secret of per-petual youth, ain't there somethin' due to their friends? I, for one, would like to witness the happy end of this love-affair, but its present progress is too slow for my mortal life. Twenty-three years to the square inch is pretty slow for a high-backed pew.

"Now, another thing. Of co'se we're not goin' to be too personal in this matter, but I'll wager right now that if we were to examine the under-side of Brother Hatfield's right coat-sleeve, we'd find it wo'e pretty thin, if not darned.

"Don't put down your knife, deacon. We

ain't a-goin' to requi'e you to show it. We ain't a-goin' to exceed the bounds of politeness.

"But I say, my brethren, I don't doubt the darn is there. An' furthermo'e—now this part I'm a-comin' to now is *a fact.* You see, Miss Euphemia is sort o' cousin to my wife's sister-in-law, so this is all in the family. An' furthermo'e, I say, my wife tells me that as an actual fact she heard Miss Euphemia wonderin' the other day how come the right shoulder of her black silk dress to wear out the way it does. She had darned it twice, an' she declared she never had wo'e the dress nowhere but to church mo' 'n three or four times in thirteen year.

"Ain't it funny to think she hasn't never thought o' the friction o' them hymn-books a-passin' over that shoulder? An' neither did wife till I called her attention to it. But she promised never to tell it. She said she wouldn't dare suggest it to her, an' so I thought, Brother Hatfield, that while I was on the subject I'd ask you, in her behalf, would you mind—as long as she has to pay for her own silk dresses—would you mind liftin' them hymn-books a leetle higher whilst you're a-passin' that shoulder-seam? Wife tells me a seam-darn is a mighty bothersome one to put in, on account of its havin' to be spliced in the middle.

"As to the wear an' tear of the top o' that pew-rail, why, I propose to refer that over to the committee on church buildin' an' repairs."

The table was by this time in such an uproar that nothing less than a response from the hitherto silent deacon could have gained a hearing.

The little man had fortunately recovered himself somewhat, and was ready to come to his own rescue with the laughing reminder that he was himself chairman of the committee on repairs, and a promise that he would call a meeting on the subject whenever it should become serious.

The deacon's voice was slender at best, but its thin, good-natured response commanded attention now; and, indeed, it went so far to restore his threatened dignity that, after a little random bantering, the subject was dropped.

But this was only the beginning. Before the next sundown everybody in Simpkinsville, excepting, of course, Miss Euphemia, had laughed over the minister's temerity, and declared it the "best joke they had ever heard in their lives"; while more than one had remarked that "ef Simpkinsville knowed what side their bread was buttered on they wouldn't let Miss Phemie get a-holt of it."

This also was the deacon's chief concern. Indeed, he declared to himself that it was the only thing he cared for in the whole affair. As for himself, he wouldn't let sech foolishness pester him into doin' any different to the way he'd been doin' all his livelong life—the way he'd been raised to do.

As he took his seat behind Miss Euphemia on the following Sunday, however, it is safe to say that he felt a tremor of embarrassment on his own account; for at his entrance there was a very definite stir throughout the congregation, not to mention the bobbing together in pairs of sundry feathered bonnets near him. Yet, even as he realized the delicacy of the situation, he could not help running his eye along the line defining the top rail of Miss Euphemia's pew, and the marked depression he saw there seemed to run in a quiver up and down his spinal column for the space of some minutes; and when, finally, in desperation, he raised his eyes a little higher, it was only to see upon Miss Euphemia's shoulder the evenly laid stitches of a careful darn.

Somehow, the silken threads seemed to raise themselves above the shiny fabric, so that he saw them clearly, even without his reading-glasses.

He knew there was no truth in the minister's remark about the wearing of his own sleeve, and he had thought him jesting throughout, and perhaps he was. Still, here was the darn. The discovery startled him so that his mind wandered during the entire opening prayer; and when, presently, a hymn was given out he became so confused that after he had presented his book—blushing, he felt, like a school-boy—he was horrified to discover that he had found the wrong place, and the trying ordeal had to be repeated. He seemed to hear the minister saying "one extry," and jotting down 12,002 in the account he was reckoning against him, as he changed books a second time for one hymn.

His state of mind was bad enough, but when he raised his eyes from his book only to see a purplish-red color slowly spreading all the way around the back of Miss Euphemia's neck—well, he could only turn purple, too.

Evidently she had heard the talk.

But here be it said that in describing this moment ten years afterwards, Miss Euphemia declared that she "hadn't heard a breath of it," and that she "didn't know, to save her life, why she had changed color that-a-way, which she knew she done, because for a second or so, when deacon passed her that book, seem like she felt every eye in Simpkinsville on her."

This seems a remarkable statement, and yet

the writer of this slender romance of her life believes it to be true, for Miss Euphemia would have died rather than verge a hair's-breadth from the exact verities in word or deed. Indeed, it seems to the writer that her subsequent conduct goes far to confirm her statement. Be this as it may, the deacon naturally took her blushes as proof of her knowledge of the affair. She not only knew it, but was sensitive on the subject. "It plagued her."

The stress of the situation was more than he could stand; and, although somewhat reassured when her wavering alto notes came in timidly with the third line of the hymn, he failed to command his own voice, and there was a clear, high tenor missing in the church during the entire singing.

He sat very still, in seeming attention to the service, until another hymn was imminent. But before it was announced the unusual stillness of his mare, tied to a tree outside the window, disturbed him so that he was impelled to go to her relief; and it was only after a prolonged and tedious manipulation of the reins that he was able to return to the church, where, instead of disturbing the congregation in the midst of the sermon, he slipped noiselessly, though by no means unobserved, into a seat near the door.

This was a definite and somewhat ignominious retreat, and so it was regarded by the delighted congregation, now on tiptoe of expectation for next developments.

If Miss Euphemia had not before heard of the minister's joke concerning her and her neighbor, she heard it now, from all sides. Indeed, before she had reached the church door to-day, one of her good friends had expressed surprise at "two sensible people like her and deacon takin' a little fun so seriously." Another even went so far as to compare the respective blushes of the two as viewed from the rear; while a third declared that she thought she'd die in her pew for the want of a laugh at the God-forsaken look in the deacon's face when he got up an' went out o' church to worry his horse.

When Miss Euphemia finally made them understand that she "didn't know what in kingdom come they were talkin' about," more than one of the good people of the church turned away, declaring they would never put faith in human creature again, and that it was a "pity some folks couldn't see the backs o' their own necks befo' they openly perjured themselves—an' in the house of God at that."

"Yes, an' looks like a thunder-storm a-fixin' to gether this minute," added a voice outside the door. "I'd 'a' thought she'd 'a' been afeerd o' bein' struck dead by lightnin'."

And still another, as the crowd passed down the steps:

"The Lord has gone more out of his way than that to make examples o' people thet set him at defiance that-a-way."

While she lingered in the aisle within, listening to the story as it came to her little by little from many lips, the color came and went in Miss Euphemia's thin face; and when she finally turned away she said, simply, though her head was high as she spoke:

"I'm sorry he troubled hisself. He needn't to've, I'm sure."

It is probable that she made no effort to be non-committal in this speech; still, taking the words afterwards, her friends found them unsatisfactory.

There was that in the mien of both Miss Euphemia and the deacon during the week following this most interesting episode that forbade any reference to the subject in their presence even by such of their worthy and intimate friends as declared themselves "jest a-burstin' to plague their lives out of 'em," and "nearly dead to know what they'll do next."

A week is a long time in Simpkinsville, where

time is reckoned chiefly either by great old clocks, whose long, ponderous pendulums seem to be lagging with the village movement, or by the slow insinuations of light and shadow following the easy comings and goings of the never-hurrying sun.

In inverse ratio to her sauntering movement is the Simpkinsville eagerness over a village event. Indeed, she is wont on occasion even to indulge in playful denunciation of her own slow pace, so far outstripped by her impatient spirit. And so, wherever two or three were congregated during this longest of long weeks, there might have been heard such remarks as the following, caught up at random during a half-hour spent in the village store:

"Well, old Simpkinsville's had a laugh, anyhow, an' it's in the deacon's power to wake her up with a weddin', ef he knows how to take a hint."

"Yas, maybe so, though there's no tellin'. Miss Phemie might take it into her head to be contrary. She's had her own way so long."

"Well, yas, maybe *so;* but I look for him to settle it. It all depends on the way he conducts hisself next Sunday. Seem like bad luck would have it thet it couldn't 'a' been settled at prayer-meetin'. We 'ain't had sech a full prayer-meetin' for many a year."

"Wife says her b'lief is thet Brother Bowen insisted on Miss Phemie goin' out there to set up with that sick child o' his, which ain't no mo' 'n teethin', jest for an excuse to get her out o' the way till folks would have time to get over this joke o' his. You see, he done the whole thing, an' he was about ez much plagued ez the next one when he see how things was Sunday."

"My opinion is thet there's some liberties thet oughtn't to be took with folks in their private affairs—not even by a minister o' the gospel."

"Yas; an' 't ain't everybody thet looks well in a joke, nohow. I never did see deacon at sech a disadvantage in my life, nor Miss Phemie neither."

"Reckon they'll be a big turnout Sunday, an' then, like ez not, Brother Bowen 'll git deacon out o' the way. Take my word for it, Brother Bowen is skeert."

"Trouble is he didn't realize how hungry Simpkinsville was for an excitement. Pore old Simpkinsville has been asleep so long thet when she does wake up she's so well rested she's ready for anything."

There was, indeed, an unusual attendance at church on the following Sunday morning, even such as were not piously inclined coming in confessedly "to see it out." While there were many who prophesied that the deacon would find the hymns and pass them over the pew to his neighbor as usual, there was not one who would not secretly have felt defrauded of a sensation if such should be his course.

There was a stir all over the church when at last the deacon was seen tying his mare outside the window. Just at this moment it was that Miss Euphemia walked calmly up the aisle, "lookin' jest ez cool an' unconcerned ez ef all Simpkinsville hadn't turned out to look at her." Such was the disgusted comment of one of her disapproving friends at the end of the service. Going first to her accustomed seat, she deliberately picked up her hymn-book and foot-stool, and, crossing to the opposite side of the church, deposited them in a vacant pew. Then she sat down. The seat she selected was immediately in front of an unoccupied one, and directly back of those assigned to the inmates of the poor-house. In taking it she had voluntarily isolated herself from any possible neighborly courtesy. Indeed, at the announcement of the first hymn, it was she who hastened to reverse the old order by quickly finding their places for both the old people who sat in the pew before her.

The deacon, who came in a few moments later than she, did not know that she had arrived until her alto voice came to him clear and strong from across the church. At its first note he reddened to the roots of his thin hair, and his high tenor, bravely enough begun, was suddenly silent, nor was it heard again during the rest of the service.

Those who kept guard over his every movement—and there were many who did so—declared that he "never even so much ez cast his eyes acrost the church du'in' the whole mornin'." Indeed, the general verdict was that under circumstances so trying, "mighty few men would 'a' stood their ground an' acted ez well ez what deacon did."

As to Miss Euphemia, there was a difference of opinion. Many were pleased to agree that she had "showed sense," and that while, in the situation, "some would 'a' acted skittish an' made theirselves an' him both laughin'-stalks, she never made no to-do about it, but jest quietly put a' end to foolishness." Others there were who took the other side, and dropped their opinions pretty freely, as a few of the following remarks, quoted verbatim, will testify:

"I don't say she didn't act ca'm, but in my opinion a little fluster is sometimes mo' becomin' to a woman 'n what this everlastin' ca'mness is."

"Why, th' ain't nothin' thet 'll draw a man to

a woman mo' 'n for her to fly off the handle sometimes, an' to need takin' in hand."

"Well, of co'se them thet don't need don't get."

"An' besides, 'tain't every woman that *wants* to be took in hand."

The truth is, Miss Euphemia's easy solution of the question that was setting all Simpkinsville agog was a distinct disappointment to more than half the village. Of course it was supposed that her action would end all talk, and things would immediately settle down into a condition even somewhat more prosaic than the old one, inasmuch as at least one hopeful situation was eliminated from it.

The dominie was, indeed, distinctly unhappy over the affair, which he insisted on considering a "breaking up of pleasant Christian relations," for which he held himself personally responsible; and he often declared to Miss Euphemia that he "would never draw a happy breath till she went back to her old seat." But this, of course, she would not do. Miss Euphemia was a woman of her own mind. She had gently, without passion or impatience, taken her stand, and in her new position she seemed, as she professed to be, "jest ez well contented an' happy ez ever."

Several weeks passed, and, excepting for the

fact that the good deacon's tenor had never been heard in the church since the day of his discomfiture, things seemed to be getting back into somewhat the old condition. Some day he would sing, and then everything would be nearly the same as before. Such was the undefined hope of the more sensitive souls among the people.

What Miss Euphemia or he felt in their inmost hearts no one professed to know, though from his silence it seemed that at least he cared a little. Possibly, if she had not cared at all, she would not have changed her seat. Or possibly, if she had cared— Who can read another, and be sure?

Sympathy was still divided, but general interest in the affair was visibly waning, when one Sunday morning the deacon, who happened to be a trifle late, walked up the aisle as usual, but, instead of taking his seat, he simply found his book, and, crossing over, seated himself quietly in the vacant pew back of Miss Euphemia. At the announcement of the first hymn he found it in his own book, and then, leaning forward, courteously presented it to her as of old.

When she turned back to receive it, delivering her own in return according to the old form, she smiled frankly in the face of the entire congre-

"HE EVEN ESCORTS HER TO HER DOOR."

gation, giving him thus her most gracious and perfect welcome.

The deacon's slender tenor sounded almost full and fine to the pleased ears of all present as it rose in modest triumph while he sang the sacred words from Miss Euphemia's book. So delighted, indeed, was every one that some of the more impulsive among them could not refrain from expressing their pleasure to the two as they walked separately down the aisle. Of course all Simpkinsville soon rang with the news, and its voice was for once unanimous in prophesying a romantic dénouement.

And who shall say that it was wrong? To whom is it given to define the border-lands of romance, forbidding all to enter save those who come in by the great thronged gate where the orange-flower grows?

Twenty years have passed since the incidents just related, and the deacon, now become an elder in the church, still sits in the pew behind Miss Euphemia, and changes books with her for the singing of the hymns; and occasionally, when the weather is very bad, he even escorts her to her door. Further than this he has never gone.

They are both old now. It is said, though it may not be so, that the deacon has recently bought a lot adjoining hers in the old cemetery. It would be pleasant to believe this to be true, and that he is pleased to wish to rest at last beside her, awaiting the resurrection. And if it be the divine pleasure, perhaps he even hopes to sit behind her in the Great Congregation, and to find her hymns for her.

THE END

www.ingramcontent.com/pod-product-compliance
Lightning Source LLC
Chambersburg PA
CBHW031926060726
47496CB00007BA/2097
* 9 7 8 3 7 4 3 3 4 8 8 2 0 *